D1123425

PRAISE FOR JOÃO REIS

"João Reis is a great connoisseur of literary comedy, in a subtle way in which everything is so natural, but simultaneously rude, with the cruel ways in which various characters are depicted, thus creating a blackly comic web that weaves together the world of the book."

—Nelson Zagalo, *Virtual Illusion*

"*The Translator's Bride* is a great little book that brings a breath of fresh air to today's moment in Portuguese literature, asserting itself as an excellent novel not to be forgotten. . . . João Reis is a perfect hybrid of Nordic with Portuguese literature. Raw, funny, twisted and melancholy, *The Translator's Bride* is a fresh breeze in the midst of the stagnant air of Portuguese literature."

—Jorge Navarro, *O Tempo Entre Os Meus Livros*

"The rise of a new voice in Portuguese literature. . . . Though influenced by Céline, Hamsun, or Kakfa, he's master of his own style and an author mostly interested in delving on life's absurdities."

—Sérgio Almeida, *Jornal de Notícias*

"A perfect short novel: João Reis does not fail. A superb book from a true writer."

—António Ferreira, *Leitura em dia*

THE DEVASTATION OF SILENCE
BY JOÃO REIS

Translated from the Portuguese
by Adrian Minckley

OPEN LETTER
LITERARY TRANSLATIONS FROM THE UNIVERSITY OF ROCHESTER

Originally published in Portuguese as *A Devastação do Silêncio* by Elsinore
Copyright © 2018 by João Reis
Translation copyright © 2022 by Adrian Minckley

First edition, 2022
All rights reserved

Library of Congress Cataloging-in-Publication Data: Available
ISBN PB: 978-1-948830-63-8 | ISBN EBOOK: 978-1-948830-86-7

Book supported within the scope of the Open Call for Translation of Literary Works by the Luso-American Development Foundation.

This project is supported in part by an award from the National Endowment for the Arts and the New York State Council on the Arts with the support of the Governor of New York and the New York State Legislature.

Printed on acid-free paper in the United States of America.

Cover design by Eric Wilder

Open Letter is the University of Rochester's nonprofit, literary translation press:
Dewey Hall 1-219, Box 278968, Rochester, NY 14627

www.openletterbooks.org

THE DEVASTATION OF SILENCE

I.

I didn't want to be there, but I was. I should have been at home, but I was waiting on a friend who'd forgotten to buy a second train ticket, he never traveled without making sure he had two, he was afraid of losing one and, if it were the only one in his possession, afraid of not being able to reach his destination, or of being allowed to reach his destination but being forced to pay a fine. Truth be told, he never boarded a train without a ticket, wouldn't dare to, much the same as he'd never been fined or kicked off, but an uncle of his had been forced to leave his passenger car once, and had spent hours at some distant whistle stop, far from any town, among the weeds and bushes, no food or water, not even a public drinking fountain, the wind bending the weeds and bushes, tugging at tree branches, and the uncle stood there until the next train came, he'd lost his ticket and had a bit of an episode when scolded by the ticket checker, who had refused to sell him another ticket inside the train and forced him off at the whistle stop after a violent argument that almost came to blows. And so, everything about my friend traveling by rail was complicated, as that was his nature: prudent. He had returned to the station and I waited for him in front of the café.

During the nearly fifteen minutes that I remained on the sidewalk, the waiter assailed me on three separate occasions to suggest the heated room in the building's entrails—a dining area for select clientele, the talk of the town in a city such as ours—and a woman tried to sell me a bouquet of red roses, she swore to me her husband was unable to work, he was an invalid, a cripple, she had been left with no option but to sell flowers on the street, she didn't have any white roses, I didn't buy anything, the woman insisted, she was pushing forty and had a sing-song voice, perhaps she also sold vegetables at the market, I stood my ground, didn't buy anything, she grumbled something I couldn't hear and departed, I continued waiting, cleared my throat, lightly kicked the steps that led into the café, the trams passed by packed tighter than sardine cans, heads, arms, and feet dangled out, the tracks shrieked, it was early morning, an unpleasant wind kicked up that irritated me, I began to feel I was coming down with a cold, my feet began to feel chilled, my friend was taking his time and I, of course, was supposed to be at home, I'd promised my wife, I'd told her I'd be back by then. I found this encounter to be deeply unpleasant, equal parts boredom and discomfort, although, if I'm being honest, I consider all social engagements to be, speaking is a lamentable act and pointless, I find social interactions deeply taxing, especially with meddlesome acquaintances like my friend, with whom, if I'm being honest, I don't speak, or at least not often—my greatest fault is that I'm a good listener, others speak and I listen, they open their mouths and a steady stream of babble washes over me, I'm a receptacle, attentive, a victim, they talk talk talk and only require my ears, then at long last, he appeared around the corner.

He offered me a cigarette as he approached, I accepted and stored it in my pocket, he let out a plume of smoke and asked me again if I remembered the day the Germans had recorded my voice. Always the same question! Without giving him an answer, I asked that we enter the café, he agreed, and soon we were seated at a table in the main dining room, not the one in back, the allegedly exclusive dining area, we didn't want to seem stuck-up, the waiter rounded on us, I ordered a coffee and my friend ordered two teas, not two teas for two people but two teas for the same person, which he required be served twenty minutes apart, so that if one got cold, he would soon have another at his disposal, and, quickly thereafter, he took a small watch from his pocket and placed it on the table, as befitted such a prudent as well as somewhat punctually perverse gentleman, as opposed to myself, who was there when I should have been at home. They served me a nice, full cup of coffee, I tasted it, found it a bit strong. Then, with the train tickets stored safely in his overcoat, my friend repeated the question he'd already asked me countless times.

Yes, I responded, I did remember the time the Germans recorded my voice in the prisoner of war camp. I assured him that, despite the circumstances, I remembered the event in great detail. One day in early June, they served us beet soup with potato skins for dinner, which also contained some flaked fish that sent the Frenchmen who ate it to the infirmary for the night. The evening was brisk, and furthermore, the soldier Almeida had died, they had informed us before dinner of his passing. It occurred to me immediately that I had in my possession a letter I had written at his request, a letter Almeida had dictated and asked that I send to his family, I still hadn't been able to mail it, I had it stowed in my pocket; truth be told, I hadn't been able to because I hadn't even tried. Once dinner was over, I left the dining shed and showed the letter to a guard named Müller, he extended his hand and remained that way, arm outstretched . . . I offered a cigarette, he didn't touch it . . . his nails grew, his fingers elongated . . . he leaned forward, stretched his splayed open palm; he would never accept something so simple as a cigarette, and, at seeing I had nothing else to offer, closed his fists and turned away.

The following morning we buried Almeida—the soldier Lopes, me, and two Belgians—we transported the body away from camp in the company of two guards, one of the Belgians spoke German and had

9

his fun telling them jokes while the rest of us dug the grave, at least the Germans laughed, they were very pleased. Even though it was still morning, we sweated profusely and there was nothing to drink, we had been given a thin and tepid soup for breakfast, lucky for me I had tucked away a kale stalk, but Lopes was subsisting only on that murky water, and, being out of sorts, saw no reason not to rest his shovel on the ground, such that it fell to me to prop him up to prevent him from falling face-first into the pit, the guards were none the wiser and the Belgian who was helping us began to dig more vigorously as a diversion; the guards didn't appreciate it when we fainted, they weren't much for productivity but they flew into a rage whenever a prisoner collapsed, the German Empire had prohibited that anyone go hungry while in its care, and far be it for them to turn a blind eye to insubordination, it was entirely reasonable, the Belgian whistled a tune and we danced on the edge of the pit, one foot forward, one foot back, and managed not to fall in. At last my compatriot regained his composure, as well as some of the color in his face, and got back to work, singing softly about everything under the sun, although more often than not about scrumptious delights, grilled pheasant with olives and nuts, Lopes had never tried pheasant, nor had I, but I would gladly have accepted some nicely toasted bread, or maybe a box of crackers, even half a box really, I would likely have been content with half a box of crackers, or three crackers and a chunk of stale roll, Lopes smacked his lips, and the Belgian, suddenly aware we were speaking of food, became curious.

"Mmm . . . *Apfel*," he said, bringing his fingers together, rubbing his belly, then pointing to his mouth.

How long had it been since any of us had seen a red, yellow, green, plump or dried apple . . . no! . . . apples were extinct, had become a genuinely mythological fruit . . . If we at least had a measly cigarette, like the ones the guards were smoking . . . Lopes continued on in his delirium.

"A pheasant, do you hear that, Captain? With a side of potatoes. Just imagine."

We finished digging the grave shortly after and dragged Almeida's body to it, the corpse was incredibly light, we hardly had to exert any effort, we flopped him over, he rolled in, and, after tossing some dirt on him, the more conversational Belgian staked a cross made of twigs at the head of the grave. It looked quite nice. We opted to rest for a while, and with our arms crossed over our shovel handles in the shade, we felt a breeze roll in from the forest, contemplated the landscape, the flowers peeking out among the green, they seemed strange, I've never known the names of any flowers that weren't roses or daisies, perhaps I could identify a tulip, but the rest, no, my memory simply won't retain them, I'm terrible with plants in general, can't tell an oak tree from a beech. Still, it was nice there, although soon one of the guards finished smoking his final cigarette, gave us the signal to leave, and we walked slowly toward camp, the Germans didn't hassle us to pick up the pace because we were so close, and, given how hungry we were, there was nowhere for us to run, the farthest we could have gotten on the soup we'd been served would have been some ten meters, to get twenty I wagered we would have required at least an entire turnip, without a turnip it was my steadfast opinion we would have been gunned down long before making it twenty meters, to make it twenty meters, if not thirty, I've no question we would've needed to consume a bowl of soup containing an entire turnip. An entire turnip! Lopes dragged his feet.

"Any word on your papers, Captain?"

I hadn't received any word and I shrugged, it drained me to

speak, Lopes wasn't quite as meddlesome as my friend in the café, but he was always asking me questions and more questions . . . I suppose I'm not too bothered by questions, the problem is that they need to be responded to, in fact, if questions didn't have to be answered, I doubt they would irritate me at all, one thing I do know, however, is that interrogations only seem to tire me because they can't be ignored, and that's a fact. The sound of our steps reverberated on the path, the breeze still felt pleasant, I thought I heard a robin redbreast. Birds are something I do memorize.

"It's sad what happened to Almeida, isn't it, Captain?"

"Yes, a shame."

"He died of pneumonia?"

"I believe so."

"He was young."

"Yes, I believe he was very young."

"Maybe younger than me, Captain?"

"No . . . I mean, yes, hmm, perhaps, indeed."

Afterward, he asked me about the possible existence of a sweetheart or wife near Almeida's home territory, and I confessed I didn't know any of those details, he was an infantry soldier, he died of pneumonia, and that was that, Lopes, for his part, would rather have met his end by bullet or grenade . . . blown to bits . . . a few pieces here, some more over there . . . one could die of pneumonia at home, and he wasn't wrong, Lopes was onto something there, it would be horrible to die of something so banal and pedestrian . . . what did your son die from in Flanders? . . . pneumonia . . . dysentery . . . the Spanish flu . . . typhoid fever . . . wouldn't be easy for a father, it wasn't an achievement you could brag to your friends about.

"I get headaches and whole-body pains, Captain. And I have sores," Lopes said.

"See a doctor, get to the infirmary immediately," I suggested.

How wonderful the robin's song! Some steps later, the camp entrance came into view, one of the lookouts had a dog whose ribs were poking out, it panted, yipped, they opened the gate following a whistle from one of the guards, Lopes stared at me, opened his mouth like he was about to say something, looked like a real idiot, then closed it and remained silent. I urged him to speak.

"Can you write me a letter?" he asked.

Yes, of course I could, all I required was that he procure me a sheet of paper, and according to him that was no problem, because he had one; it was never clear to me where they scrounged up these sheets and scraps of paper, some didn't even know how to read and yet they managed to come up with writing materials faster than I did, it was a mystery that only proved what I lacked, they were clever, possessed practical knowledge and the know-how to put it to use; they were illiterate and rich in paper, and I, a paperless good-for-nothing . . . We walked on. I couldn't hear the robin redbreast anymore.

"I want to tell my dear mum to sell the sheep if she needs money. She gets attached to the animals, it gets expensive."

I assured him I would write the letter that same day, perhaps before dinner, but never after, no, it was best to write before eating, because it helps with digestion, and in our age of abundance one can never be too cautious about digestive health. That made him very happy and he grinned, Lopes couldn't have been more than twenty-three and had worked in the fields with his father before being recruited, he assured me often that it was better to handle a hoe than a howitzer and I believed him, I also imagined him carrying a sack of potatoes on his back, boiled potatoes, fried potatoes . . . a potato feast!

After we passed through the gates, Müller approached me, stated that Commander Schiller wanted to speak with me, and, ergo, that I should make my way to the Kommandantur, shovel be damned. The sky was blue and the sun radiant—a perfect day.

The gossip in the barracks was that Schiller had a sister near Munich to whom he sent portraits of the prisoners, it was also rumored he'd wanted to be a painter, but had been kicked out of the Academy of Fine Arts, that the art world had crushed his dreams, that his creative ambitions had perished due to something involving insults and a duel over honor, the outcome of which was his joining the military—high drama for such a noble spirit, Schiller was an artist, all one had to do was look at him to see the spark, there was no doubt about it, that man was born to create, the army had broken him, I saw no reason not to believe it was all true. He was seated before a backgammon board when I entered the room, he rose and I saluted, Schiller ordered the guard to leave, we seated ourselves and he struck up conversation, luckily, Schiller spoke excellent French, we understood one another easily, and without moving his eyes from the papers spread over his desk, he spoke at length on the necessity of remaining vigilant against the misplacement of official military documents, didn't refrain from referencing the corrosive effect of French and Belgian soil on paper, which was in stark contrast to the effect of peat and wetlands on corpses—something I was likely familiar with—and he added as well that he had taken my situation into consideration, as well as my request that my case be resolved, but that he was at the mercy of the circumstances, and, ergo, there was nothing left for him to do but await receipt of the documents from the competent military authorities, however, the telephone lines were cut, there was bread strewn across the roads, and grain still to be harvested . . .

the Portuguese command didn't respond on Sundays and, for financial reasons, also refused to employ the postal service . . . not a single official seal . . . not even a stamp . . . and they had already eaten all the pigeons in Germany . . .

"*Mein Herr*, it would bring me great joy to see you transferred to an officers' camp, but, as you surely understand, I simply cannot make an exception and accept, without proof, not even a nameplate, your supposed rank as captain. You understand, don't you? Please be sympathetic, *mein Herr*, war requires patience."

Afterward, he told me to keep in mind that the fight marches on, that it is interminable, that the patient man is the man of the future. Patience pays, he said, he assured me that the man who waits is invariably compensated and went on to explain that there's no greater virtue than patience. He inquired if he had ever told me the story of his disgraced cousin. He hadn't. He stretched out his legs and rocked back in his armchair a bit, I thought for a moment he might jettison himself onto the floor, but no, he didn't, he remained seated; I believe he even gave a little hop in his chair.

"My cousin was a very impatient young man. Some years ago, he dated a girl from Westphalia, all in secret, of course. One day, the girl lied to her parents and went to meet him on the sly, they spent the afternoon together, you know how it goes. At the end of the day, he accompanied her to the station and watched her board the train, but he was in a hurry . . . I don't know if he was meeting another woman, if he was hungry . . . but he put the girl on the train and walked away, you see? He'd left his handkerchief with her, however. When she realizes this, the train is already leaving the station, and, without thinking, she throws herself off the car, handkerchief in hand, slips off the edge of the platform, and falls in a heap on the tracks . . . it was like a sheet of paper passing through a sewer grate. She ended up with her head yoked between the tracks, how embarrassing!, handkerchief in one hand, and my cousin nowhere to be seen! All because the man was impatient. As was she! Ergo, you must understand, *mein Herr*, without papers . . ."

Although the story was cryptic at best, I understood it perfectly, I couldn't be sure whether Schiller had made it up or not, nor what his intentions were in telling it exactly, but nevertheless, I understood, yes, I understood, because I am perceptive, and he was right, I didn't have any papers, they had stolen them during our surrender, along with my coat, my gaiters, the watch my father had given me, my money—they were confiscated, not stolen, one must be precise, they confiscated them because I was a prisoner of war, they told me, and due to my being a prisoner, they said, they were duty-bound to confiscate my belongings. The German uniform they gave me wasn't my size, the sleeves were too long, and it was too short at the waist: my deformed torso resembled an inflated bellows. An aberration, certainly, but not surprising in someone with an asymmetrical body such as mine.

"Shall we have a game of backgammon?" he asked.

I agreed. When we finished, Schiller ran his fingers through his hair and proposed a second match, a third, I won them all quickly, during the fourth match the commander began to huff and tug at the ends of his ginger mustache, he kept it very straight and sharpened the tips with wax, it bore a slight resemblance to emperor Wilhelm II's mustache in the portrait Schiller had hanging on his wall. I let him win. I felt good there, as I did in the forest, silence was the silver lining of being interned, no machine guns, mortars, or stray bullets, only the occasional gunshot, an increasingly frequent nap-of-the-earth flight . . . aerial battles overhead . . . I enjoyed the comfortable, silent repose, and, a few moments later, during the fifth game, Schiller's cat wriggled through the slightly open door, it was an orange cat, furry, we not infrequently spotted it crossing the yard, it rubbed itself against my legs, I scratched behind its ears, it slinked forward and leapt away, only to return soon after, no, no, it had no fleas or lice, Schiller made sure of that, an orderly combed it daily with three different combs in a dignified spectacle to behold everyday around three in the afternoon, after which the orderly would remove the fur from the different-sized teeth and toss it into the yard for the wind to catch like a child making soap bubbles. The commander stroked his luscious mustache, twirled the waxed ends, straightened them, pulled them to their limit, felt satisfied, the cat drew nearer to its owner, Schiller delighted as soon as the animal leapt onto the table, outside, the racket continued, you could see them through the high window, heaving two massive wire spools toward the front of the Commander's residence between gasping breaths.

"Pardon me," Schiller said, coming to stand with the cat in his arms and heading toward the door where, moments later, he summoned the guard, they exchanged some words, I remained seated at the table, Emperor Wilhelm eyed me suspiciously, I thought I saw his eyes glint behind the glass, and on the desk, beneath some papers, I caught a glimpse of Schiller's famous sketches, they weren't bad, the portraits, and when he returned to the table, I inquired:

"Do you have a portrait of Almeida?"

"Ahlmaida? Who is this Ahlmaidaaa?" He stroked the cat.

"The soldier who died of pneumonia yesterday. You might remember having ordered his burial this morning."

"Ah . . . I'm not sure, I don't know him by name. There are so many men here. So many men! Ahlmaidaa, say it for me . . ."

He tried to pronounce the name correctly. I repeated it slowly:

"Al-mei-da . . ."

Schiller couldn't hack it, his tongue lolled around in his mouth . . . he even went so far as to stick it out at one point.

"Here, *mein Herr*, look at this. It rolls up."

It was enormous, and did indeed roll up . . . how scandalous . . . his tongue was filthy . . . officially disgraceful . . . Schiller didn't remember Almeida . . . My god, there were hundreds of prisoners. He did confirm, however, that it was possible he had drawn him, he expressed that perhaps he had sketched him, it's not out of the question, he assured me, that he had done his portrait. Perhaps during one of his morning strolls through the camp, or if he had caught a glimpse of him during formations, who knows? Yes, it could be, insofar as his face might have drawn him in due to any number of characteristics. Was this man cross-eyed, squinty-eyed, or big-nosed? I tried to remember Almeida's face as he laid on the cot in the infirmary, or when he requested that I write the letter, but I could only remember him in the yard, his face turned down, bowl in hand, on one of the occasions when the soup had spilled. I didn't say anything. At that moment, the cat meowed, and Schiller attempted to console it. Failing to, he became irritated and paused the incessant stroking of his mustache.

"You see, Commander, if you so happen to encounter—"

"*Mein Herr*, without papers there's simply nothing I can do. Afterward, perhaps, I can have you transferred to Breesen . . . and there you'd have your own orderly. Until then, however, my hands are tied! There is work to be done. I have more problems than I know what to do with . . . this camp is always in the midst of some crisis . . . Because of the prisoners, only and entirely because of the prisoners! And the Russians, have you even stopped to think of the Russians? We have to feed them when they wander in here. Or would it be better to let them starve to death, *mein Herr*? We are civilized men, are we not? It is no easy task being commander, let me assure you of that . . ."

Not easy indeed, I stood up and saluted him, the commander called the guard once more, and he escorted me to the door. Before leaving, Schiller asked if I had anything else to say, I didn't, I wondered for a moment if I shouldn't air some of my other grievances, the prisoners going hungry, for example . . . At the end of the day one expects a bit more from a captain, from a military officer of rank, yet I turned my back and abstained from speaking because it is my belief that silence is invariably the best option, I have found that there is no better response to any and all problems than not speaking. Outside, the two reels of wire were abandoned in the yard in front of the Kommandantur, and the men had gathered in groups a few dozen meters closer to the barracks. The sky continued radiant.

Corporal Timóteo sang and danced in the middle of a group of Portuguese soldiers, he was the only soldier in the camp who had served under me, he danced away his sorrows and the lice soared from his head . . . it was full, absolutely chock-full of them . . . the other men paid no mind, however, because if it wasn't lice it was ticks, a little blood, a lot of blood . . . those were the battles we had left to wage. Even so, I feared one of the German soldiers would see him in such a state, which would unquestionably lead to a general disinfestation of the entire camp, as well as a mass depilation . . . it would be, however, difficult to hide it from them, as there were enough lice in that camp to suck half of Germany dry, and all it would take would be the flight of a single louse catching one of the Germans' eyes . . . I therefore intervened, in an attempt to calm Corporal Timóteo and move the men to a more private area.

"So, Captain, are the Krauts going to transfer you?"

I shook my head and told them no: No papers, no rank. They

smiled and tried to cheer me up, perhaps because I was a little down, or appeared to be, I'm not quite sure, one of the men proposed we play cards to pass the time and I accepted his suggestion under the condition that we not wager food, as the grilled pheasant had left me unwell. Meanwhile, some of the Frenchmen had made their way toward the group, we assembled a surface out of a broken-down crate, and, when we were finished, there were four of us standing around the improvised table, Corporal Timóteo and I made a pair, Lopes joined up with Le Bidon, the latter wetted and smoothed back his hair . . . I eyed his nits. Another den of infestation. France was making short work of Germany in those days . . . oh, yes . . . They proposed bets, Timóteo wanted to wager half a serving of dinner soup, perhaps we'd get sausage, a nice addition to the pot, I grew incensed and gave the crate a whack, almost split it down the middle, I thought I had been clear in saying we would not be playing for food, that I didn't even want to hear mention of it, it was repugnant, Lopes suggested we bet the bunk, a pallet bed made for one, those who lost would sacrifice their bed for a night, during which they would sleep on the floor, each loss would equal one night, however, Le Bidon, being a Frenchman, didn't sleep in our quarters, they separated us by nationality at night, when it was too dark to tell us apart by our features or the tilt of our mustaches. We were faced, therefore, with a slight problem, due to which I found myself obligated to explain to Le Bidon the details of Lopes's proposal, he smiled and stated he would wager an hour of work for each game, an hour that would be completed regardless of the tasks involved . . . including cleaning the toilets . . . the latrine pits . . . if he won, one of us would take his place . . . I translated the Frenchman's gibberish and the men appeared satisfied.

I entreated everyone, however, to move from behind me, I didn't want anyone at my back, I never wanted anyone at my back, I always took that precaution, that of not having anyone behind me, especially during war, because being a good officer requires always being attentive to your rearguard, there's no future in the military if you don't know who's behind you, I'm quite sure a soldier wouldn't hesitate to skewer us with his bayonet or shoot us in the back for being an officer, or club us in the head even, I was sure that in the absence of witnesses, a soldier is perfectly capable of letting us have it from forehead to skullcap with the business end of a bat, or if not, of slitting our throats from ear to ear, it seemed to me it was in their blood after weeks, months, years of authoritarian oppression, I too, while we're on the subject, wouldn't hesitate to kill a large swath of superior officers, I concluded it was in our nature, that men are men because they can kill with pleasure or indifference, that man is nothing more than a violent monkey whenever he finds himself free from the binds of society, which is why crowds are so dangerous, they'll string you up without batting an eye, those soldiers were the masses, war is waged by the masses that desire our elimination, each face in the crowd belongs to an assassin, I gestured for the prisoners to move beside me and the game began. My cards were terrible, Timóteo's too, we lost the first hand, Lopes and Le Bidon wasted no time in celebrating . . . they reveled in their victory . . . the Frenchman shook himself and the skinfolds that hung from his chin waggled to and fro . . . a veritable dewlap . . . how awful . . . I turned my head, the June heat was stifling and I sweated profusely, I felt thirst prodding my tongue, but I had left my mug in the barrack and didn't want to ask a fellow inmate for his, illnesses ran rampant in the camp, tuberculosis and pneumonia were our silent killers, I had been told that the winter before, the Romans had died from the flu by the dozens, I was still far away at that point, in the trenches, when the Romans were dying by the shovelful, that's what they told me, that the Russians had perished by the hundreds from dysentery, all number of lip and tongue pestilences were most certainly also present . . . pustules . . . open sores . . . cracked skin . . . better to remain prudent!

My mind wandered and the men grumbled, soon I owed Lopes another night on the pallet bed and a second hour of work to Le Bidon, we began the third hand, the Frenchman could barely squat under the burden of his own weight, he had been in the camp almost since the beginning, and the degree to which he had retained the lard around his midsection while the Portuguese soldiers, who had only been imprisoned for a matter of months, were slowly withering away was inspirational, the food wasn't enough to sustain a man, but, of course, Le Bidon wasn't quite a man . . . he was a beast . . . Moreover, he possessed a wide range of attributes, some mornings he was no stranger to the trafficking of goods . . . tobacco . . . paper . . . crackers . . . socks . . . women's clothing . . . Given the amount of soap that passed through his hands, you'd think he'd find the time to wash his hair, give his scalp a good scrubbing, perhaps throw in a little garlic and vinegar, too.

"Captain, why aren't you playing your hand?"

I had been eyeballing Le Bidon's nits, I quickly tossed a card down, Timóteo had something to say about it, and rightfully so, because we lost the hand, losing displeased me, it's true, Le Bidon and Lopes rejoiced, and I turned away to shield myself from the degrading spectacle of the dewlap once again . . . from one side and then the other . . . When the celebrations subsided, I requested a rematch, they accepted, the circle around us drew closer, the men let loose their grunts and heaved sighs, it made the hairs on my neck stand on end . . . I felt them grazing my nape . . . I was almost at the point of jumping up and shouting "Get out!" but the game continued, the cards proved far more forgiving, we won, Timóteo was all hot air, we had regained two of our previous losses and soon he was bragging as if we had the upper hand, I tried to calm him down, was unsuccessful, and the disturbance attracted the attention of two of the guards, among them Müller, who waved his hands wildly and ordered us to disperse while the men shrank back and protested. Among the confusion, Timóteo hid the cards in his pants and we disbanded, the Portuguese to one side of the yard, the French to the other, and afterward, every man for himself. Timóteo continued following me, struggling to run with his pants dangling loosely from his belt.

"Wait, Captain!"

His cries fell on deaf ears and I walked on in the hopes he would desist, I began to roam far from the barracks and tents, people annoyed me . . . questions, conversations . . . all pointless, inane . . . I yearned to hear a robin again, or a blackbird, it was hot, a crow squawked. Along the barbed wire to the North, I noticed the soldier Ferreira, better known as "Slingshot," who held in one hand the item to which he owed his nickname.

"Captain, Captain, onward, my captain," he stammered, then halted.

He wasn't the sharpest tack, some of the men had fought with him in Flanders, where Slingshot had gotten lost from his post during a counteroffensive and, under the distant watch of his compatriots, wandered for two days through the trenches without ever daring to peek his head out in order to run to friendly lines, until the Germans finally spotted him in a communication trench and began using him for target practice, a role he managed to escape by throwing himself into an enormous missile-blast crater where he spent another day, this time among corpses, severed limbs, and two injured men who moaned through the night, and where, after both had gone silent, he found himself alone the next morning as a gas bomb went off, he fled at long last, with no mask at all, and only stopped running when he collided with two members of his own company. He lost his vision for four days and never again spoke a single word that made any sense. Made sense to us, that is, at least to us . . . did it make sense to him? It's possible . . . even probable! Despite his feeble mind, however, he had fashioned a slingshot out of a twig and two clamps he'd found God knows where, quite a feat, and he carried it with him everywhere; the Krauts found it comical and saw no need to remove it. When he opened his closed fist, I worried he was hiding another slingshot, but it was only a snail.

"Captain, onward, my captain."

Then, he shoved the creature into his mouth and chewed; he preferred his snails served in the shell.

"Captain, onward, my captain."

At least that's what I understood of his drivel . . . he spat . . . his mouth was full . . . a beast . . . an animal! . . . innocent, however . . . I agreed and Slingshot saluted me; I carried onward, and he continued saluting as I took my leave.

I had taken my leave. I decided to sit behind the kitchens, some Brits and a few Russians were circled around the trash searching for potato skins; one extremely tall Russian, a skeleton really, found half a beet and quickly consumed it, it stained his face and hands, he roared with laughter and seemed happy, his companions found it infectious, I think I even smiled.

I wanted to write, to commit what I was thinking to paper, what had happened in the camp that day, but I chose not to, I didn't have any paper and besides, it was pointless, a waste of time, I contended myself with listening to the birds instead, but I couldn't hear the robins' song. It was too early, they were resting in the trees. To my side, the Russian hopped about with his chin painted red.

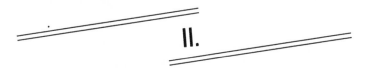

II.

Later, they served us potato stew with melon rinds. We gnawed on the rinds a bit, and a few men found fingernails in theirs and were forced to gnaw harder, I, for my part, had already digested my dinner and was reviewing the letter, as there was nothing else left to read, we'd eaten the final pages of our Bible the week before, stewed up in a helmet with water and nettles. I'd asked the camp chaplain, Howard, for a new Bible, even a small one, told him any version would do: Catholic, Lutheran, translated from Hebrew, Arabic, perhaps in French, or German . . . My English was almost perfect . . . fluent . . . I'd put my knowledge to good use, I still remembered my lessons with my dear preceptor and there'd been no lack of practice in the trenches . . . I understood Howard easily, however I found myself compelled to answer him only in French . . . a personal affectation! After all, I had to keep expectations low.

"Do you confess to have strayed from the teachings of our Lord and Savior?" he asked me.

"*Comment donc!* Yes, I do, of course," I admitted.

Subsequently, I fled. Regarding my post-dinner reading, the deceased Almeida hoped the missive reached his dearest Lúcia in good health, both her and her loved ones, he had written her with the help of a captain who was also imprisoned there, he reported that the conditions in the camp were the same, not much food, that was his only complaint, but, well, it's better to eat little and survive than to be in the trenches where you don't eat much and also die, he was eating better now that he'd been hospitalized, he had a fever and it was hard to get out of bed, but he didn't want her to worry herself because the doctor and the nurses were taking good care of him, he hadn't been maimed, his body was still whole, he would love to hear how Lúcia was doing, what she was doing, if she was taking the firewood to mother or helping her with the stove, he dreamed of seeing her again, as soon as he returned home he would take her to the ocean, she'd never seen anything like it, the ocean is beautiful, and so vast, on his trip to France it seemed it had stretched on forever.

It was incredibly boring reading. I folded the paper, first in half, then in fourths, I had also written the letter Lopes had requested, asking his mother to sell the sheep if money was tight, which is obvious, and of course to rest at the end of a long day, so as not to work oneself to death. I stored his letter in my pocket alongside the previous one, Lopes trusted me, he was as convinced as the others that I would be able to send the letter off without issue and that I would receive a response, I was a captain after all, Schiller held meetings with me, we played backgammon, sometimes even checkers, there was no way the letter would be confiscated by the authorities, that was the belief they all held . . . they were sure of it, all of them, as if it were a religion and I, the Portuguese army's sun-god, their apparition in the trenches . . . a phenomenon to boost candle sales . . . high quality candles, no less . . . a serviceman with a halo around his neck . . . a light squeeze, a little cranial compression . . . the enlightenment of fasting . . . I had achieved levitation, no longer had any use for walking . . . or eating . . .

Not everyone slept easily that night, Timóteo lay on the floor, Lopes was stretched out comfortably on the pallet bed, the trades and arrangements had been made, as per usual Costa's feet weren't bad company, I had grown accustomed to their smell, had developed a bit of a habituation to them, wouldn't even have had a problem eating near the stench, I guaranteed my friend in the café that it was, without a doubt, possible to eat in the presence of foul odors, one simply had to become accustomed to them, even in the presence of a rancid smell, I assured him, it is perfectly possible to enjoy a meal.

Some of the men spoke of women, others of food, those were the only two topics ever discussed, one of them swore to us a woman had winked at him and offered him some bread on our most recent work outing through the village near the cannery, she was German and blonde, some twenty years old, still rosy-cheeked and with good meat on her bones, she'd been a heavenly vision, she'd winked at him, and not because she had something in her eye. Ah, more drivel . . . His bunk mate believed the part about the wink, but not the part about the bread being offered, there was simply no way it could have happened, it was unthinkable to offer bread to a prisoner of war, even just a chunk of it, and it was white bread no less . . . yes, white bread of all things, impossible, there wasn't white bread anywhere in all of Germany, in all of Europe, maybe not even in Switzerland . . . at best it had been sawdust bread, or sand and gravel bread . . . and, indeed, he hadn't brought the bread back with him, had he . . . did he eat it in the village, in front of the Germans? According to him, however, there was a very simple explanation: the guard hadn't allowed the woman to give it to him, he had struck him with the butt of his rifle and shooed the woman away, and she ran across the field as the guard stuffed the bread into his own pocket, curbing forever their blossoming affair. It was certainly food for thought . . . The conversation quickly turned to Schiller's sister, the camp's shared object of desire, the soldiers had lost countless hours describing what they would do to the sister of Schiller, that pig, the bastard left us high and dry, his cat ate more than the entire battalion, his sister was blonde, brunette, a redhead, tall, short, skinny, fat, each imagined her to his own liking, I envisioned her blonde and blue-eyed because I prefer brown-eyed brunettes. Soon after, for lack of another subject, they settled for venting their frustrations at the rations we'd been served in the trenches, as well as the constant delays in food delivery. Truly a scandal! One soldier, whose name I can't remember, stood up from his bed and began to shout:

"The bread was this big! This big!" and exhibited his raised pinky finger for all to see.

We had no choice but to agree . . . the bread had not been sizeable. That was the only possible explanation for why we had been captured by the enemy, that we were weak from hunger. Costa considered such commentaries unfair, obscene, a real stab in the back . . . the ingratitude . . . he had performed numerous food deliveries, had carried the bread slung over his back like a cartridge belt, the soup pots clutched between his hands, he would enter through the communications tunnel, climb the trench and run through an open field on whose opposite side, at the enemy's frontline, a Kraut would catch him in his sights, and as soon as he pulled the machine gun trigger, Costa would be forced to dive into the first hole he could find. He spilled the soup all over his pants on one occasion, but it hardly mattered because he had also pissed himself, and the bread was in an even sorrier state than he, as it had taken a tumble in the dirt . . . alas, a day like any other . . . Moreira from the 5th Infantry had complained at first, but he ate the dirt-covered bread and assured Costa he'd never tasted anything so delicious . . . it was all factual,

not a single lie had been told . . . Needless to say, the entire barrack was in stitches, but he couldn't have been less interested in their
opinions. And there was more! On another occasion, mortars had
begun to fall all around him as he was carrying provisions, there was
smoke everywhere, he heard screaming, they had set off gas bombs
and Costa was forced to put his mask on as the Germans advanced
full force, while at the same time the Brits, who hadn't calibrated
their artillery, directed their fire at allied trenches; the provisions fell
in the mud, Costa spun around, ran through the trench, lost what
remained of the food along the way, threw himself to the muddied
floor, buried himself beneath the scattered bodies and shoved his
hands into their hot, loose innards while he waited for the enemy to
move on, then heard us retaliate against them through a confusion
of smoke, random shots, and cries. He barely managed to lift himself
and, with cleanliness in mind, ran off in search of some water to
rinse his hands, he found a canteen, washed himself, and, at the end
of the afternoon, from among the moans of the injured, overheard
an officer shout:

"Where's the son-of-a-bitch who didn't bring us any food, huh?
Who was it? I'll kill him!"

Immediately after, the same officer grabbed a rifle and attempted
to fire it into the air, he needed to calm himself down, the rifle was
jammed, however, and a soldier shouted to him:

"It's the sand here, it gets into the breech and then into the barrel,
jams the trigger . . ."

"The only breech I know is your mother!" the officer responded,
wasting no time in procuring another rifle from the ground and trying to fire it—nothing, it was also jammed . . .

The officer grew enraged, threw the rifle against the wall of the
trench, the butt slammed against the rotting wooden panels and the

impact loosened the weapon's trigger mechanism, which fired and struck the officer squarely in the neck. They called for the stretcher bearers, who failed to arrive before all of the man's blood had drained into a viscous puddle, and Costa demanded to know what good it did to complain about a lack of provisions, as that was how you'd end up, hungry and dead . . . there was no use blaming the transporters . . . this wasn't a grocery store! Everyone's got their own problems! Costa didn't want to hear anyone complaining about a lack of provisions on the frontlines, and in any case we were all prisoners by then, war for us amounted to a flea- and lice-infested barrack, there was nothing left to gripe about, what remained for us was to practice patience . . . all signs seemed to indicate that patience was the best option . . . from what I had observed, to weather life in the camp, one required a stoic disposition. Minutes later, the men returned to the topic of Schiller's sister. I was tired and hungry, dinner hadn't sated me and I tossed and turned in my bed, the taste of the melon rinds that overflowed from the soup pot rose into my mouth, I swallowed the bile, the rising stomach acid, and stared at Costa's feet, which disgusted me despite my newly acquired habituation, his toes rose and fell like out-of-tune piano keys, only his big toes stayed rigid, I yawned, but I didn't sleep because I was addressed by corporal Timóteo.

"Where'd you hide your wedding ring, captain? Did you lose it?"

I noted the silence that fell over the barrack, it was far too hot inside and the men panted, the mosquitoes buzzed, Slingshot quietly barked, "Captain, onward, my captain" from his bed as he tried to squish the insects with his hands, and then with his tongue . . . it protruded from his mouth like a camel's . . . truly a beast . . . I turned to Timóteo, he pointed to the mark on my finger, a spot much paler than the rest, I covered my hand, they were no better than a gaggle of church ladies, ignorant and meddlesome with their endless questions, a complete lack of social graces. It seemed that Lopes awoke at that same instant and asked me:

"Captain, where would you like to be right now? Home?"

I propped myself up on my elbow, Lopes did the same, forty prisoners breathed the musty barrack air in silence.

"If I could choose, I would be lying in the grass in Papua New Guinea, taking in the fresh air," I answered.

They had never heard of Papua New Guinea. I thought of telling them the stories of my ancestors who had sailed near there, my grandmother's stories, recounted by the fireplace, the old woman used to teach us our family history, that glorious past, she would talk until she fell asleep and sometimes she'd get startled, let out a shout, swear that she'd seen a rat run across the room when in reality she'd only caught a glimpse of a strand of her own hair hanging over her face . . . Those stories, hours wasted on conversation! In vain! And for what? I considered speaking to the fact, but I refrained. The less we let on to those around us, the better. A closed mouth! Since they missed their cabbages, however, and their cottages by the river, they forced me to explain what the other side of the world was like and if it was possible to reach it by any means other than being shipped off to a penal colony . . . some way that didn't involve deportation . . . I found myself once again between Costa's feet . . . oh yes, I was fine with the smell . . . One of the men's uncles had been sent to Timor, he'd begun life as a typesetter and ended it as a convicted forger and deportee, he'd gotten his start falsifying signatures on checks and promissory notes, and by the end was printing his own bills, a talented artist. Eventually he was exiled. Lopes wasn't convinced Papua New Guinea was located near Timor. I didn't mention the cannibals or the Germans that existed there, and they seemed to enjoy the sound of the word Papua, they repeated it endlessly, Papua . . . Papua . . . Papua . . . it certainly was a land of exotic birds of every color and shape, rich in plant life, lush forests, flowing water, an abundance of food . . . Costa quickly got to imagining Schiller's sister in a crystal clear spring, nude, her hair cascading down, his Helga . . . she embraced him as he dove into the lake. They asked me further details and I supplied them. Once again I omitted the Germans, why bring it up?, I told them there were villages there inhabited only by women, where they allowed only one man entry who stayed for half the year, the other half he spent in another village, it was paradise, a personal harem, I told them, in these villages one man had forty or fifty women at his disposal, I assured them, it's an entire village for just one man, I said.

They quieted down. I continued my story—pure fiction—without offering any personal details, solely to entertain, I didn't have anything to write on, after all . . . I had no materials . . . I tried to give it some flair, but I'm no storyteller, no, I'm simply an attentive listener, my voice began to falter, weariness returned, I recalled the ocean, my house, I closed my dry lips, a stupor spread across the barrack and I closed my eyes to rest in the lull that, at night, halted the devastation of silence.

III.

The next day began quite pleasantly. The soup was somewhat thicker than normal, it had pumpkin rinds and even a chunk or two of actual pumpkin in it, and the only disturbance of the morning came from the Russians, whose demand for a second serving devolved rapidly into a hullabaloo, the guards intervened, however, and after a few whacks from the butt of a rifle the men grew calm and everything returned to normal. The silence that followed was marvelous, albeit brief, and I quickly caught up with a pack of Frenchmen, as it had fallen to me to settle the lost bet and fulfill an hour of work for Le Bidon, who had just disappeared behind the barracks with Müller, only to reappear soon after, cigarettes in hand. I asked him for one, he grumbled, I asked again, he acquiesced, and I stowed the cigarette in my pocket.

We were in no hurry, a dozen men, myself included, had been digging a trench, a pit for the western wing's latrines, which had wasted no time in overflowing, we rested often on our shovels, with preference for a spot of shade, my hour of work had almost ended and Le Bidon smoked above us, we were stuck up to our knees in the mud, and, to the left, a French prisoner scratched himself, lice, most certainly, which is how we were when we overheard shouting, an altercation coming from behind the kitchens. Le Bidon ran toward it, his lard bouncing . . . a horrific sight . . . it seemed impossible and against the laws of nature that he could move so nimbly . . . how grim! . . . his legs were like two hams in motion . . . starving, we followed after him. It was so appetizing I began to salivate . . . A few meters later, I spotted a number of my compatriots surrounded by four Germans, and Timóteo drew near.

"Captain, they beat up Slingshot, he's all mashed potato!"

It was true, he wasn't mistaken, at the center of the closed circle lay Slingshot, his head in a pulp, his utensil motionless on the ground beside him, what a mess . . . it was difficult to ascertain exactly what had transpired. Schiller's cat had disappeared, hadn't spent the night in its basket in the Kommandantur, and therefore Slingshot, who put everything in his mouth, must certainly have eaten it, which,

as is customary, led to a prompt investigation. He had demanded to
see his captain, which had led them to kick him bloody, and, soon
thereafter, Müller had plucked his eyes out with his bayonet before
beating his brains out with the butt of his rifle and the help of a colleague. Slingshot hadn't made a peep.

"He didn't even cry for his mother?"

Not a single scream, they told me. We were somewhat puzzled,
and, shortly thereafter, Müller ordered us, his arms aflutter, to
clear away the corpse and *Raus!* We were curious where we might
take it and Müller suggested the infirmary, it was indeed a location
like any other, I gave Le Bidon a signal, alerting him I wouldn't be
returning to work at the latrines as my hour had already expired,
and joined the group; we wrapped Slingshot's head in his tattered
coat and headed for our destination, four of us carried the cadaver,
it wasn't very heavy, Slingshot must have lost weight recently, his
head quickly drenched the coat and our path was soon marked by
leaking trails of blood, each drop a piece of Slingshot soon to dis-
appear into the earth, had we crossed all of Europe, we would have
ended our journey with arms loosely swinging, and, thanks to
Slingshot, the marigolds would have sprouted, he'd have merged
with the tributaries of the Rhine, the Danube, and fertilized all the
grain in France. War permitted us moving flights of imagination,
even without stepping foot outside the prisoners' camp.

Slingshot's head hit the stairs leading into the infirmary numerous
times as we arrived, each new step was marked by an accompanying
thud, in the atrium we were received by a nurse who directed us to
a room, we placed the corpse in it, I held onto the coat, the head
appeared unrestrained and soon to fall off, we didn't want to get the
floor dirty, there were no shenanigans in the infirmary. A little while
later the doctor emerged, agitated and shouting in German. Upon

seeing us, he mixed in some French and English words, the result of
which was an unintelligible gibberish, I sought to understand him,
given that the others were scratching their heads and shuffling their
feet, and for good reason! The doctor, a lieutenant, was furious, he
wanted us to move Slingshot to a table, I tried to explain that he was
dead, but he didn't appear to grasp the circumstances . . . I chose
instead to show him Slingshot's head . . . nothing more than a bloody
pulp, a deformed mass at the end of his neck.

"*Ja, ja.*"

At last the doctor understood his patient's condition, and quickly
slammed the door as he fled the small room along with the rest of us.
He followed behind us as we ran. With the doctor at our heels we traversed the long hallway that bisected the infirmary from end to end,
there were beds scattered here and there occupied by patients suffering from pneumonia, tuberculosis, gonorrhea . . . a medical school
. . . advanced anatomy studies . . . all very bizarre . . . I glimpsed
a Russian who, while plowing the fields near the prisoners' camp,
had rested his hand on the rails so the train would sever it on its
way by, in the hopes of being repatriated to Russia once and for all,
it seemed to me he never would have put his hand on the rails were
it not for the opportunity to be sent home, and, in that case, would
have remained in possession of both hands, he sighed often and was
a sympathetic fellow, perhaps somewhat melancholy and, as of that
moment, wasn't going anywhere, he waved to me with his remaining
hand and I returned the gesture. My three companions dispersed,
they immediately struck up conversation with the patients, and I
accompanied the doctor, whose name was Lang, he escorted me to
his office, a small, dark room, we entered, Dr. Lang requested that
I help him complete the paperwork, transcribing Portuguese names
was troublesome. I seated myself at his side, I felt good in his office,

serene, Dr. Lang conversed in a heavy but fluent French regarding
the advantages of being a doctor in a prisoner of war camp, one
didn't come across quite as much mutilation as in the trenches, ampu-
tations were less frequent . . . However, the principal advantage, and
one that he had achieved by being transferred to his home region,
was that at the end of the day he was able to cycle home and into the
open arms of his wife and children, I imagined a Hans and a Helmut,
perhaps a Helga with blonde braids, Dr. Lang was blond, blue-eyed,
couldn't have been more than forty, which led me to imagine his
children as blond, as well, and possibly sadists, ah yes, he had the
face of a sadist, was most certainly a pervert . . . he also had a horse
. . . in truth, it belonged to the regiment, but due to the food short-
ages the commander had authorized him to take the animal to his
small villa, where he fed him leftover hay and oats.

Dr. Lang told me this while I helped him fill out the papers, he
was a friendly man, although his exhaustion was apparent, the Germans had the war by the hairs, he said, he guaranteed me they were
eager to return to peacetime and get on with their lives, they would
much rather be tending to their businesses, he declared. Take his
father-in-law's tobacco company, for example, whose empty Hamburg warehouse he owed to the attacks and seizures of barges in
the Atlantic, his only recourse had been to dismiss his employees,
at home they rationed bread and butter, Lang, who, as a lieutenant, had access to the camp provisions, was the only reason they
didn't starve, it was clear the knave had been helping himself to
our potatoes and turnips, completely understandable, the Germans
were inundated with so many gunshots and explosions that they
woke us up in the dead of night with their screams and bugle blasts,
their clarinets in the bell tower . . . every geezer too old to serve in
the military had a bugle or harmonica, he told me, they hung them

36

around their necks and really had at it, their baseline volume was extremely loud. He admitted that at the beginning he too had been drawn in by it all, had let himself be swayed by the newspapers' effusive headlines, the patriotism above all else . . . indeed, he had personally engaged in a beating, with the help of some others, of a man who hadn't sufficiently taken up with the crowd as a parade for the Kaiser and his men-at-arms passed by, the man had seemed content to stay seated with a napkin tucked in his shirt, scarfing down biscuits and tea, wouldn't you rather join in, they had asked, and what's the score here, but the man had remained reclined in his chair until they kicked him out of it, perhaps he had been a spy. He had certainly deserved it, or at least the doctor had later deemed it so because, at the time, he wasn't entirely sure . . . That event had disturbed him, it was clear . . . they'd left the man in a sorry state, his glasses smashed, his tie torn . . . Lang didn't have anything against the French, you see . . . that's how little control people had over themselves . . . he even knew the language, had studied medicine in Paris, was a student of the great master, Dr. Leclerc-Armand, the famous Dr. Leclerc-Armand, the venereal disease specialist . . . and as for the economic losses, what would his father-in-law do with the men whose arms Lang had amputated? A man with no arms in a tobacco warehouse? What kind of a silver lining is that! Would he only lift one side of the crate? A disaster! Some portion of what nature had generously granted the Germans had been lost in the wartime din, my God, what happened to solidarity among men? Afterward, he swore to me somewhat abruptly that the bees in Berlin are the softest in all of Europe . . . the entire world!, he all but shouted it in my ear, the situation disturbed him, they stored all the honey away in caves to rot, only consumed synthetic honey now, which was all chemicals and noxious to the intestines and stomach, it was the gall bladder that suffered most . . . The list of drawbacks, ergo, was vast. Not to mention the rationed butter . . .

But that I shouldn't say anything of what he had confided in me to my peers, that I shouldn't get the wrong idea . . . since I didn't even speak German . . . a miscommunication could easily occur during my conversations with Commander Schiller, who was ever attentive to signs of dissatisfaction or insubordination . . . Lang was a nervous fellow, one could easily have pushed him up against a wall and ordered him to fire, despite the fact that he was only a doctor, when the fact of the matter was that he enjoyed the utmost comfort the war had to offer, four walls and a roof overhead instead of a tent, a shack, a hovel in the mud. He was in an infirmary many miles from the front, gone were the days spent meandering through the trenches, everything was clean in the prisoners' camp, even if the fleas and lice ran rampant, he inquired as to whether I incorporated soap into my bathing routine, he was curious to discover if it could eradicate the pernicious pests. I was sorry to disappoint him, but I hadn't used soap on my hands since I'd been captured. Dr. Lang inquired as to my origins, the war gave him a rare opportunity to get to know men from distant lands, he'd had the opportunity, for example, to examine Senegalese men, Congolese men, and men from villages whose location he would be unable to pinpoint on a map . . . the largest hurdle of his career thus far, accustomed as he was to a more pallid, Teutonic complexion . . . He was never quite sure if his German patients were dead or simply asleep, he would check their pulses . . . ice cold . . . a setback he'd grown accustomed to . . . But now! It was fascinating I'm sure . . . Lang was also anxious for the future opportunity to examine a North American, he informed me, he had crossed paths with numerous Portuguese, some had died, others not. What was there for me to say? Nothing! Silence was always the best option . . . I took a couple steps backward, positioned myself closer to the wall . . . Much safer there! Prior to the war, Lang had met one of my compatriots there in Germany, he was a driver for a factory owner the man had recently lost track of, however he was an exceptionally enjoyable gentleman, his judgement was perhaps clouded, he did indeed possess some unusual habits, during the event in question the Portuguese man had parked the vehicle he was driving, opened the door for the proprietor, and, seemingly out of nowhere, ordered his boss to sit in the driver's seat and take the wheel, the boss's jaw dropped, he was baffled and unmoving, dumbstruck, so the Portuguese man closed the car door and took off, leaving the old man stranded on the sidewalk with nothing to do but watch as the exhaust trail grew and grew. That compatriot of mine was a man of vision . . . very impressive for someone from such a small country . . . I felt enlightened. Lang wished to examine a specimen from such a peculiar race . . . I recoiled backward, blurted something out . . . And when nothing more spilled forth, Lang deduced from my silence that I was reserved, timid. Use my words for what? My mouth was closed, my character uncompromised! I was honing my silence . . . What could I tell him about my life? That as a civilian I had been an engineer? That I had also studied in France? Under the engineer Mersault? That I didn't have enough paper with which to write? Trifles . . . He shrugged his shoulders and continued speaking, eventually offering me a cigarette, which I gladly accepted, I came forward a few steps, it felt good to be in his office, Lang seemed to have forgotten his work, perhaps he had nothing to do, and I was in no hurry, I would only be able to eat some hours from then, the doctor, however, was permitted lunch and consulted his watch, Slingshot's paperwork had been filled out, the German had also undertaken to fill out the death certificate. Cause of death: head trauma. It checked out.

"Shame about the cat."

A shame, indeed, Schiller was likely deeply perturbed, Lang anticipated a possibly drastic measure, despite the fact that, by contrast, the lieutenant doctor appeared quite pleased by a piece of news he had received some days before. It would appear that a commission of German scientists was to visit in the coming days, with the mission of collecting data on the myriad languages and dialects present among the vast selection of prisoners across the dozens of camps—phonologists, linguists, anthropologists, all of them delighted—Lang thought of recommending me to the specialists, I could recite a poem, sing a song . . . Well, why not? As long as I didn't have to talk too much . . . We would see, provided the right moment arose. As for Slingshot, little more was said and we headed back toward the room where we'd left the body.

In the hallway we crossed paths with my countrymen, the nurses were tending to the patients, many of them involved in attempts to communicate based largely on gesture . . . they were laughing, had each other in stitches, it was a veritable bacchanal, an orgy of disinfectant, ether, and ligatures . . . upon opening the door to the room, I noticed Lang hadn't removed the coat from Slingshot's now-gelatinous head, certainly fortuitous, because if he had, the floor would have been covered in blood by then, most unfortunate. We searched Slingshot's pockets but found no letters, photographs, nothing, I removed his boots, put them on, my own footwear had long since expired, they fit, Lang kicked my old boots into a corner and I searched again for any vestige of Slingshot's civilian life, however without success, Lang told me they would take him away once they'd gathered the two Englishmen who'd passed away at dawn, they seemed invariably to die at daybreak, he had yet to pinpoint the cause, they'd spend all night in agony, crying, writhing, insulting their homelands, laughing, oh yes, they would be seeing their neighbors again soon, they were on their way home, the war was ending . . . only to return to their curses and damnations, an entire night spent shouting and raging, all so they could kick the bucket at daybreak; luckily in camp they died largely from pulmonary illnesses, lacked the lung capacity for grand digressions, and therefore ended their lives in greater peace. Certainly a relief. However, one never knew quite what to expect from the calmest of patients. Some, in a final act of defiance, and seemingly only to perturb the medical staff, shat the bed just before departing.

"Do they cry for their mothers, Dr. Lang?"

Lang smiled at my question, he too had reflected on the need to cry for one's mother at life's end, as the suffering finally claims victory over the body. He asked himself if madness was a prerequisite to preventing a patient from calling for his mother at the hour of death . . . At this point I was no longer listening. I was hungry, a little delirious, my stomach was growling, Lang's findings would have sat with me better were I also privy to a nice lunch, I didn't need an extravagant feast, anything would do, yet he continued on with his nonsense, to hell with that conversation, there I was clinging to the doorframe in order to keep myself upright and that son of a bitch was off rambling about a mother's uterine role, the comfort known only to the unborn . . . he should have been having that conversation with his wife, at home with Hans and Helmut, they had something to eat even despite the rationing, what did Slingshot and I have to do with any of that? Nothing! Couldn't a man ask a simple question without risking being subject to a litany of garbled French contemplations, and in a dreadful accent to boot? The conversations, the questions that illicit responses, the unnecessary words . . . What was necessary was to eat, yes, I intuited that I had a headache from the hunger and that the day had already ceased to be as enjoyable as it had been when it broke, the doctor carried on in his elucidations, and in that moment I wanted to die, to never have existed, but, truth be told, if I wanted so much to die then perhaps it wasn't necessary to eat, I was so hungry, however, that all I could think of was eating, and I wasn't able to think of dying at the same time, even if it was to my advantage not to eat in order to attain my goal. My head grew full with those painful thoughts, and I clung harder to the doorframe.

Lang eventually quieted down, I righted myself and followed him, we traversed the hallway again, I asked him for another cigarette, he procured it—I would say unhappily—and I once again had tobacco trapped between my fingers. The topic of conversation had changed, he had returned to discussing the delegation of scientists that would carry out the survey of the camp's foreign tongues, it was likely they would arrive shortly. I indulged his observations and reconfirmed my interest in offering as much help as possible; there was nothing more to say.

With the nurses absent we were left only with the wounded and infirm, the doctor and I sat on the edge of one of the beds, it looked to me as if the patient who occupied it had been bandaged from head to toe, he had suffered burns moments before being captured, Lang informed me, a grenade explosion near a gas tank. It seemed perfectly possible it had happened that way.

"It's a miracle he survived," Lang said, "truthfully I'm not sure how he's still breathing."

We each lit a cigarette, the Russian and I, there was no shortage of Russians around those parts . . . Lang bored me slightly, but he offered me cigarettes and it was hot outside, I clung to the hope I might be privy to a portion of his meal, he had a double, triple ration . . . He insisted once again that I verify my past, where I had lived, where I was born, if I was married, if I had children, parents, what my profession was. My God! In lieu of an answer, I asked him whether he had ever visited the officers' camp and if they screened films there, according to the rumors they were afforded ample libraries, French novels, theater productions, I should have been in one of those camps. The doctor confirmed that rationing was occurring across all the camps, both those for officers and otherwise, even if the top brass enjoyed more comfortable conditions you shouldn't count on an officers' camp having an abundance of food, he clarified, the officers have also been forced to go without. And, speaking of food, it was Lang's lunchtime.

As we said goodbye, the lieutenant doctor counseled that I come to the infirmary more often, perhaps he could guarantee a small improvement in my living conditions by having me admitted, even if on fictitious grounds. They always ate a bit more around there. I promised him I would, we clasped hands; Lang departed, and I continued hungry.

Once outside, I sensed a certain agitation in the air. Still somewhat woozy, I joined the Portuguese soldiers, who, same as the rest, had placed themselves in formation and, without delay, I was brought up to speed by my compatriots. Schiller was about to conduct prisoner reviews. All around us, the guards scrutinized the line-up, there were only a few of them, the important ones, our old friends, one of the German soldiers was sporting a pair of glasses he was always taking off to clean, he'd lost minutes, hours buffing those lenses, had a habit of loudly accusing them of never being clean, and, whenever he saw the Englishman he'd confiscated them from, would give him a whack for keeping such filthy glasses. Old habits, I suppose. Another guard not infrequently used a sheepskin cloak, one of the coats our government had thought to send us so we might pass the previous winter a bit more comfortably . . . they had made us instant targets of ridicule in the trenches, the enemy erupted into fits of laughter whenever we passed by, we were sheep stuck in the mud and the barbed wire . . . a moving field of snow. A shocking sight! And sound! The Germans bleated at us . . . a sensorial onslaught, all things considered . . . Nor did our allies hesitate to join in on the fun at our expense . . . The Brits even went so far as to construct a target out of some of the coats and use it for rifle practice. In the field, the Germans had quite a time engaging in pranks and surprisingly believable sheep imitations. Truly embarrassing.

I lined up behind Marques, a telegraph operator of low stature on whose head the lice squirmed to such an extent I was compelled to shift my gaze . . . Schiller, however, was already examining the formations from end to end, his face puckered, trembling, he began to swear and, upon passing my section, pointed ostentatiously at the telegraph operator's head, he was irascible, the fury was rising to his scalp, his skin was turning red, I couldn't make out everything he was saying, only a word here and there, but it quickly became obvious we were in for a general depilation.

"*Schwein*! Idiot," Schiller said as he hit Marques. ". . . *Zás*, I'll show you . . ."

He really let him have it, the commander, it was quite memorable, no one would have thought he had it in him . . . Marques paid sorely for the lice . . . he certainly also paid for the cat, the bedbugs, the war . . . And rightfully so!

A commotion began to arise among the prisoners, I heard

grumbling, objections, not due to the aggression against Marques, but due to the depilation, they wouldn't quiet down, dammit, I couldn't hear a thing! The guards punched one or two of them, however, and peace reigned once again. Afterward, and with some effort, I managed to hear the Frenchmen's interpretations, the depilation would begin at that exact moment and would commence with the Portuguese soldiers, and thus it fell to us to direct ourselves as soon as possible to the barracks; the other prisoners dispersed, within the group around me were already being uttered the foulest obscenities, the beds were quickly unmade inside the barracks, and, while everyone was occupied, I hid the letters, my box of matches and my pencil stub beneath a floor board, then we exited, scant bedsheets in hand, and, at the door to the showers we undressed, leaving our clothes in a large pile, the first prisoners entered a few at a time, each one covered in dye by a hunchbacked Russian holding a bucket, a toothless Russian who looked shockingly like a rolled up slug . . . the saprophyte unfurled his body upward to stain our hides, I waited my turn, looked around and noticed we were becoming increasingly more bone than skin, a natural phenomenon, perfectly understandable, even advisable perhaps . . . the Russian laughed at our wholesome, communal nudity. I, however, didn't fit in, I stood out in my strangeness, my body was asymmetrical from the shoulders down, one side significantly shorter than the other, not from the war, no, no . . . That's how I was, uneven, lacking in symmetry, a doctor had confirmed it to me in my infancy, and now, in adulthood I remain the same, although seated and with a coat on my lack of proportion is hardly noticeable . . . it might seem to be a case of only minor importance, however, experience has taught me that it is not: faced with my physical constraint, it appeared I might have hoped to avoid military service and masculine comradery, and for a while I did, I studied civil engineering—civil, not military—I hadn't wanted anything to do with the army because of my physical proportions, as well as for other reasons, largely because I never liked having armed individuals behind me, but alas, I was rounded up as the country readied for war, I thought my deformity might have deemed me unfit for a military career, it wasn't a pretty sight during the medical inspection, repugnant in fact . . . but unfortunately my father had intervened, as was his habit, and pulled some strings . . . he sent chouriço and paio and broa de milho to certain individuals and I transitioned from civil engineering to military, to officer, to captain . . . Without any aptitude, of course! I would have preferred to draft projects from my desk or at a hotel table, but we are all defenseless in the face of familial ambition . . . And so, there I was, standing silently before a bald, toothless, hunchbacked slug, curling somewhat forward so as not to shock my countrymen . . . it was important to maintain discretion, to not attract attention, that was always the best practice . . . The Russians who worked the showers gathered up the clothes for disinfestation and griped immediately upon seeing the bloodstained fabric and squished lice. All we could do was let them talk and they quickly grew tired . . . one of them attempted to continue but lacked the strength . . . Afterward, once we were all inside the building, they began the depilation, it was quite horrific, we looked like plucked chickens before going under the shower heads, I, however, looked more like a crippled garganey, deformed poultry, the cold water wounded our skin like tiny grenade shrapnel, the fragments of the German *potato mashers* that penetrated us in a thousand tiny wounds. We'd fallen out of the habit of bathing . . . some of the more prudent among us had never bathed to begin with . . . the prisoners fled from the water . . . the Russian who doused us at the entrance laughed, what a

beast! The lice soared, the fleas as well, almost as high as the ceiling
. . . they too craved freedom, dreamed of it at night . . . it was their
right, after all . . . they were up in arms. They didn't want to live in
barracks either . . . Eventually the prisoners began laughing and at
such a volume that the Germans entered the building to investigate,
one of them, a corporal, fell face-first on the ground and the guf-
faws grew deafening, although they quieted the moment the corporal arose, as silence is always the best response . . . The corporal
refused to admit defeat and, coat and pants soaking, stalked across
the showers, I withdrew, I hadn't even been laughing, it wasn't in
my nature, but I was asymmetrical!, stares fell to me naturally, I had
known it since infancy, if there was someone to single out, the asymmetrical fellow was always the first option, with one side shorter
and more slender than the other, he must certainly have something
to hide or be guilty of a crime, I told my friend in the café it wasn't
paranoia, the problem hadn't only begun during the war, no sir, this
problem of mine was real and very old, even as a child I was the
center of attention, I was timid, withdrawn, and yet they insisted
on observing me as carefully as possible, out of so many millions of
men, among so many thousands of fools and scoundrels who don't
deserve to be living, I was always the target . . . if I ever found
myself in the presence of a hunchback with two humps, then perhaps
I would be spared . . . or someone lame . . . But, in the absence
of hunchbacks or cripples, it will always be me. Even as a boy
. . . my peers would skip school, and at times our teacher wouldn't
notice their absences, I, on the other hand, was called on every day
because of my asymmetry . . . with a pain in my heart . . . it was
food for thought . . . the teacher didn't call on me maliciously, yet it
was impossible not to notice my withered left side . . . even if I sat
silent and stationary in my chair, without moving a single muscle,

which helped me to acquire a certain steady-handedness that has proven indispensable to my career . . . The corporal drew near and stared at me from a few centimeters' distance, because I was nude I made unflinching eye contact, he wanted to see if I would laugh and I gave him nothing, not even a blink . . . I was used to it, had extensive experience . . . Eventually he desisted. The guards left and the prisoners returned to their festivities, as did the fleas, the prisoners soon began laughing again, my stomach cried out in hunger, which is why I didn't laugh, I thought only of eating, of nothing but food, my companions were likely also thinking of food . . . that was my hope, that perhaps they hadn't noticed my asymmetry, perhaps they were hungry and only thought of eating, the corporal included . . . given the rationing . . . I leaned on the wall and tried to spy the forest from the window.

IV.

My friend raised his voice in order to be heard above the mob that had invaded the café and ordered a third tea, the first two had chilled, he wasn't interested in hearing me talk about my asymmetry, it perturbed him . . . moreover, seated in the café, my deformity likely appeared irrelevant . . . to him and to the waiter. He, with his teas and his watch, had never been to war, didn't know how horrendous the food had been—oh, that soup! He'd been stuffing himself scrumptiously while we in the camp sipped that thin, murky liquid . . . He was only interested in particular stories and, according to his watch, he had time . . . the train would only depart on the following day, and he planned to leave his home three hours prior to the hour listed . . . He was able to make plans well in advance, quite the opposite of myself, who, ever since being incarcerated, am only able to conceive of the present, I fell out of the habit of making plans, a habit which, when you really look at it, is truly disgusting: we make plans and yet we die without getting back the time we lost planning how to fill the time we didn't live, it's disgusting—making plans is, in the truest sense of the word, heinous. My friend asked me again if I remembered the exact day the Germans recorded my voice, if I was sure I remembered everything, I guaranteed him that yes, he had only to wait a little while longer for me to recount this particular episode, that I would tell him the whole story. Resigned, he shrugged his shoulders and offered me a cigarette, I accepted it and stored it in my coat pocket.

The air in the barrack weighed heavy and stagnant, our skin was still sensitive from the depilation and we had been entertaining ourselves with stories of peacetime, one of my compatriot soldiers had once seen a goat with three horns, and when his grandfather was young he'd had a cow that gave birth to a two-headed calf, one body with twice the amount of head, from its neck protruded double the head that should have, a phenomenon which attracted visits from the entire parish. Stories, and then, more stories . . . Another soldier had become fond of a woman on a train once, he simply had to go to one of that woman's parties, he never would, however, because one year from that moment, as we were at last being repatriated, he would be dead, crushed by a crate thrown overboard, but, as he was still alive and didn't know he would be killed by a crate that would one day fall from a repatriation vessel, he asked if we were familiar with *The Guide for Affable Men*, a book he'd purchased during his travels; he knew how to read, a rare treat.

"What's in this guide?" one of the other soldiers inquired.

"Everything! But mostly how men should speak to women."

"And how should men speak to women?"

"Well, in order to even think of speaking to a woman, the man should weigh at least twenty kilos more than her and be fifteen centimeters taller, or else . . ."

"Or else what?"

"Things will go south, and their children will come out deformed. But it's rare they'll even have kids, because if you aren't twenty kilos heavier and fifteen centimeters taller, it's likely there's nothing doing."

I tried to ascertain if my father weighed twenty kilos more than my mother, and a barrack mate asked me if I'd like to play a round. The nights were terrible, during the day we were occupied, but at night we got to thinking, picturing food, our houses, food again, painful memories from our childhoods—that abominable era— would mix with images of food and our torture would grow and grow, I recalled my impotence before the plate I was ordered to clean, the impossibility of choice in a world into which I had been thrust unwillingly, war was indeed an extension of the torture of being born . . . that was what I was thinking, and most certainly others were as well, though perhaps in different words, with less clarity and cognizance, they rambled on about two-headed calves, but their minds turned to the pain of entering the world, they grew distressed and some even cried, but only to laugh soon after. Later, they cried more. What was worse, however, was the sound of grumbling stomachs, the growling innards, so loud we had to pause until it subsided. Our stomachs were on the warpath, it was the rebellion in the viscera . . . Once the wailing ended, however, everything carried on more smoothly; it was quiet, and one could sleep.

For dinner we'd had soup, beans bobbing atop a fatty liquid, not the worst, by any means. At that moment, my legs and head itched, the men were still speaking, detailing what they would do to Schiller's sister, and the bunk was mine, given that Costa had dragged his feet to the ground; he enjoyed playing cards as much as I did.

"Care for a game, Captain?"

"Yes, I think I would," I told him and jumped from the bed, which squealed.

"Le . . . le . . . le . . . t's shu . . . ffle the deck."

"Pass it here."

"I . . . I . . . I'd like to see if you . . . you . . . you d . . . d . . . do it better than me."

The solider, named Fonseca, had a stutter like machine gun fire, taaaka-taka-taka, bullets flying overhead . . . Costa shuffled the deck, Timóteo began to speak of his concertina, and how nice it would be to have it there with him, he asked if I was glum, if I was feeling sick or sad, but nothing could have been farther from the truth . . . I felt great, what did it matter whether I was happy or sad? All that mattered was ingesting that soup, opening wide, shoveling the food in, swallowing, and shutting up. Perhaps I seemed depressed, I opened my mouth and soon closed it . . . Timóteo, on the other hand, took every available opportunity to sing and dance, he was a happy fellow, some men are like that, I had already written two letters for him, one for his wife, the other for his mistress, he loved them both equally, it was quite moving . . . He winked at me and did a jig, it sickened me deeply, the pretense of intimacy was vile, the grotesque gestures repugnant, from within his winking eye I saw the ignorance of an entire people, decades upon decades of ignominy, lack of culture, perversity, gluttony, incest, infanticide, leprosy, scurvy, syphilis, I chose to ignore him, as I already had the cards in my hand.

"You . . . you . . . you . . . you . . . you're hi . . . d . . . ing cards up your sleeve" Fonseca said moments later.

"What did you say?" Costa's voice rose.

"You ... 're ... pu ... tting car ... car ... cards up your sleeve!" And Fonseca slammed his own on the ground.

A commotion ensued, we paused the game and separated the men, it was understandable, after all, we were gambling for a safety pin. The uproar didn't subside immediately, however, and the sound was such that two guards burst into the barracks, almost kicked the door down and shouted *Ruhe, Ruhe*, the prisoners settled themselves, the Germans wanted to know what could possibly have caused such a racket ... they were a refined and orderly people! Sargent Bartz, who knew very little French, twisted his mustache as he spoke, it was curious, he used almost as much wax as Schiller, I was startled by the quantity he'd applied ... I didn't know how he twisted it if it was sealed in that way, it looked like yellow-painted stucco—Bartz was blond, his hair and beard were blond.

"*Was? Kartenspiele?*" he shouted.

"*Nein, nein!*" I responded, pointing quickly to the safety pin ... Bartz half-closed his eyes and turned up his nose ...

"*Herre Gott!*" he said.

I remained somber. Bartz laughed, and, afterward, went silent, I crouched down and grabbed the safety pin; as I arose with it between my fingers, I felt the eyes of each of my colleagues fall to me.

"Here it is, sergeant" I said to him in French.

"*Danke!*" he said politely.

The sergeant was dumbfounded, the prisoners as well, they had no idea what was happening ... but restlessness and the rustling of tattered clothes soon followed ... thump-thump-thump ... heads bumped against cots ... fleas leapt through the air as if they were trying to jump higher and lay down at the same time ... Bartz's stucco mustache rose, descended, returned to its original position, the Germans took down my prisoner number and left under the weak light of the oil lamps, through the window, you could still make out a rosy sky to the west, it was still daytime in those parts. I laid myself down to rest.

The barrack was silent and I tossed and turned in my bed, Costa had already lain down, someone sneezed, I overheard a barely whispered "fucking Krauts," followed by a sigh, then the creaking of wood, I felt tired, my innards churned, my stomach cried out, I tossed and turned then stopped, grew still, a man burped in the semi-darkness . . . Disgraceful! Abominable nights, difficult digestion, the body wasn't made to process kale stalks and bean skins . . . The rose-tinged westerly glow faded outside and I returned to the window, I felt uncomfortable, decided to get up, and, despite the noise I made, no one offered a word, I put on my boots, opened the door and exited, I breathed deep, we were fortunate, Schiller hadn't decreed a curfew, one of my peers was in another prisoners' camp and their commander, some Manfred something or other, made them lie down unfailingly at eight o'clock, daylight or not, and they were forced into it by whips, hard canes, branches . . . cruelty, in summation . . . yes, our camp was fortunate . . . I walked a bit, tiny bats tried to capture insects and a few swallows still crossed the sky, no robins, however, all that was to be heard were the steps of a few sentries and the sounds coming from the latrines, where prisoners entered and exited, as well as the barking of a dog, the guards did their rounds, the air outside—which was free of the human musk of the barracks— was pleasant, reinvigorating. I headed for the latrines, lighting a cigarette along the way, my last, property of Dr. Lang, it occurred to me that I might ask him to send the letters for me, Almeida's and Lopes's, after all, he was a doctor and a lieutenant, a German with blond offspring and a wife at home, a horse that ate oats . . . What might Lang be doing while I entered the latrines with my cigarette between my lips? Perhaps he was lying with his wife, his Helga, the father-in-law asleep in the guest room, his sacks of tobacco—the remnants of his warehouse in Hamburg—atop the mattress, and the children dreaming in their beds, the horse, however, likely slept standing, one ear raised against intruders out for its oats . . . oat soup with nettles, snails, frogs, the works! . . . one must remain in a constate state of awareness during wartime . . . a country at risk demands it, after all . . . We were on the cusp of a new era, fated to confront the future and mold to it to our desires, the war to end all wars, the final battle for a better Humanity.

I seated myself on an open toilet. An empty stomach fills one's head with delusions, strange images, I looked to the sky and then at the beams that served as dividers, and there I saw two Englishmen and a Canadian, they waved to me, seated on the latrines, they spoke to one another and traded food, crackers for cigarettes, cigarettes for slices of bread, I thought I caught a glimpse of a slab of butter, chunks of cheese, a key lime pie, there was no limit to what those pockets could hold . . . were they military pockets, or civilian . . . ? We must have found ourselves at the precipice of a new stage of human development in the face of such pockets, never again have I seen pockets of the kind I saw during wartime, these days we can't store much more than a key ring and a handkerchief in our pants, much different from the pockets of the time, out of which bread, ham, bottles, pulleys, and lice emerged . . . I crossed my legs, smoked my cigarette to its end, and stared at them, it wasn't worse there than in the barracks, one only had to grow accustomed to a different kind of stench, some moments later a patrolling guard gave us a frown then departed, and the others picked up their conversation where they'd left off.

I recognized one of the Englishmen, he was not my biggest fan, his name was Williams, I remembered him perfectly, he was still sporting the same hairstyle, the same uniform as well, though slightly more worn, I'd had an altercation with him in the past, a quarrel, if you will, we were billeted together in France, quite far from the frontlines that stretched across some hills, advances and retreats of just a few meters occurred almost daily and the British command was receiving dozens of complaints from the French villagers who lived nearby. The townspeople certainly had reason to be outraged, they were unquestionably beset by inconveniences, the Portuguese had been running down their chickens on the side of the road, trapping them beneath the wheels of their cars and trucks, cooking them in large skillets or in cans, the Brits, however—who received provisions, care packages, photographs, locks of hair, and offers of engagement—had no way of understanding, it seemed an unsurmountable task for them to perceive this was no large emergency, and an irrational and imprudent misunderstanding had begun to arise between us . . . I suppose they had their reasons, given the galloping speed with which military pockets were evolving, the progress really was staggering. One of the British lieutenant colonels intended to present a grievance to our Portuguese field commander, had made up his mind to make a mountain of a molehill, I had accompanied him in his car, which was driven by an orderly, and that orderly was the man seated on the toilet in front of me, none other than Williams himself, his own spitting image, though a bit grayer, he was slowly flickering out . . . Williams the Candlelight . . . During the journey, the lieutenant colonel hardly opened his mouth, the orderly, however, never seemed to close his, the Portuguese were this or that, they were dirty, illiterate, absolute idiots, the sheep brigade, a military freak show, fodder for the cannons with their tattered clothing and rifles that were always jammed, they didn't have gas masks or ships, no vehicles or horses, just a few starving asses the French chose to sell instead of butcher, we were, in his estimation, the laughing stock of the entire Western front, and, to top it off, racially inferior, short and hairy, almost simian, to put it bluntly, we were half-breeds, demonic, a fleet of hearses that all stunk of garlic . . . I made a point to note I was no shorter than he, much less was I illiterate, and I certainly didn't stink of garlic . . . I was perhaps more irregular, more asymmetrical and, certainly, somewhat hairy, but not shorter, no . . . our pockets were also equally vast . . . Soon, we came across some British infantry soldiers signaling to us and flapping their arms, we ignored them, the discussion and the car carried on, Williams took his eyes off the road, and, around that time, the lieutenant colonel attempted to speak, he'd already zipped past a few more infantry soldiers gesticulating along the roadside, I spied smoke in the distance, the blackness stretched out before us, and then, an explosion erupted in the roadway and the vehicle was ejected into the air, did a turn and a pirouette, and, by the time I knew what was happening, I was stretched out in a field, my uniform covered in sod. After some effort I rolled over, and, when I arose, saw the car. The vehicle had flipped over, the wheels, now facing the sky, were still moving, and smoke rose from the projectile in the road, Williams found himself kneeling a scant few meters away, and the lieutenant colonel moaned from beneath the vehicle, I drew nearer the latter and the orderly soon followed . . . the officer's legs had been crushed, his pants torn all the way up to the waist. I glimpsed part of his groin, a none too uplifting sight . . . Together, Williams and I tried to liberate the lieutenant colonel, pull him from the debris, albeit without success, he groaned grotesquely, and it wasn't long before the bellowing began.

"Just hang on, we'll get you out of there" said Williams, who was doing laps around the car, the lieutenant colonel cried out in pain, though I don't recall if he called for his mother, because shortly thereafter I spotted the German artillery.

"Listen, Williams, the Germans are on their way."

"Yes, yes, let me think, let me think!"

I walked to the road, my kidneys hurt, I felt some pressure in my back, still today I feel pain in my kidneys when it's humid, my kidneys alert me to any change in temperature, whenever it rains the pain spreads to area the behind my belly, quite a nuisance, the lieutenant colonel, for his part, screamed unceasingly and a projectile struck a tree some one hundred meters from the site of the accident, I brought my hand to my forehead and scanned the horizon, it was infested with tiny men, horses, and combat vehicles, behind them loomed the outline of an enormous cannon, one of their Big Berthas, a true metallic monster.

"The German artillery is closing in," I said.

"I'm thinking, goddammit!" Williams retorted.

Williams thought. The elder Englishman grunted hoarsely from beneath the car, I crossed the road, the other side of it was also agricultural fields, a small house peeked out from the middle of the field, now in flames, the artillery advanced down the road and, in the lead, a lancer rode atop a horse.

"Williams, we must beat our retreat post haste"

"But . . . but the lieutenant colonel is trapped beneath the car. I can't leave him here . . ."

"Listen, the Germans will take care of him" I told him. "They'll capture him and take him to a hospital, then they'll transfer him to an officers' camp . . ."

It would be simply wonderful, I guaranteed him, but he was not convinced . . .

"Your officer is the most fortunate man among us: as far as he's concerned, the war ends today! Goddammit, there are laws in situations such as this, Williams. What do you think this is? We're all gentlemen here! Your colonel is a lucky man, believe you me. He's not going anywhere, he's nice and safe, observe."

I punched the car.

"We, on the other hand, have to beat it if we don't want to be blown to bits by Big Bertha."

Hesitant and bewildered, Williams wandered between the road and the car; the lieutenant colonel whimpered and contorted himself, but only from the waist up . . .

"The lieutenant colonel, the lieutenant colonel, what will happen to the lieutenant colonel . . ." recited the orderly.

"Remove me from here, Williams . . . get this thing off me . . . I order you not to let me be taken by the Krauts, Williams." Then he groaned, he was certainly not out of breath.

The looming figure drew nearer, I decided to position myself closer to the car.

"I'm leaving, Williams; are you coming or not?"

"I'm going with you, I'm going with you . . ."

"Williams, don't leave me here, I implore you, on the lives of whomever you hold dear back in England, on the lives of your family, your country . . . the king . . . don't toss me to the Krauts on French soil, Williams. Not on French soil . . . My God, French soil, who would have thought . . . ! That's an order, you hear me, you must remove me from here, even if you have to carry me on your back . . . I'll have you court martialled, Williams, you can be sure of it!"

"Lieutenant colonel, I don't know how to get you out."

"A lever, Williams, a lever! What are you waiting for? Ask the Portuguese for help. Is the Portuguese there? I don't see him,

Williams, I don't see him . . . and on French soil . . . ah, it doesn't hurt anymore, I can't feel my legs, my God . . ."

The man was entirely obsessed with French soil, and that Portuguese officer of his, the miserable fellow . . . although my preference was for French, my English was immaculate, I had understood everything he'd said perfectly . . . if the war had lasted a bit longer, today's world would likely be full of polyglots with bottomless pockets . . . we would all carry our supermarket purchases in them, and spend our days removing handfuls of beans and chickpeas, grips of sugar, and salt to taste . . . the world would no longer hold secrets, we would switch between tongues with perfect ease and even a certain measure of cleanliness!

On the other side of the road, a giant projectile had just launched some earth into the sky, and, like a volcanic eruption, embers of carrot showered down, Williams grumbled, shook himself off . . . Through the dust, the sod, and the carrots I glimpsed again, from afar, the German lancer on his horse who marked the front of the forces that had broken through our lines, he was heading in our direction, I circumvented the car and stared at the British lieutenant colonel, who looked back at me with a defiant air, wriggling like a larva, it was a very indecent display.

"Remove me from here. Go on, pull me. Pull me up, man . . . What are you waiting for? Come on! Are you an officer or a rat?"

The car had crushed his legs, it would be impossible to remove him or transport him the entire way back to headquarters . . . what a nuisance . . . The Germans neared, the lancer was advancing slowly yet inexorably.

"Remove me from here, I order you both."

Williams stared at me and I grabbed the lieutenant colonel's ceremonial saber, which had fallen to the ground beside him.

"Here, have your saber. Let's go," I said. Williams agreed.

"You can't leave me alone in this state, in this predicament. I order you to rescue me! My God, I can't feel my legs, I can't feel my legs . . . on French soil . . ."

Either way, he was doing just fine, as far as he was concerned the war had come to an end, the two of us, however, were preparing to run out of there when we heard the horse drawing nearer, it was moving at a gallop now, the lieutenant colonel moaned and elaborated on the mineral properties of French soil . . . I set myself to listening, the horse had stopped trotting and I saw the lancer's helmet crest above the side of the car like one of the many treetops on the horizon, projectiles fell all around us, although with decreasing frequency, the air filled with smoke, and at my side Williams grabbed his pistol, I did the same, the lieutenant colonel whimpered. I gave Williams the signal to move around the car, one on each side so we could outflank the German, he waved to me . . . each took his path around the overturned vehicle and we confronted our enemy, who had dismounted and was holding the horse by its reins, he looked at us aghast, perhaps he wasn't expecting two men, perhaps he was only expecting one man, or even no men, he pointed his pistol at me, extended it as far away from himself as possible, and I aimed mine in return. The German lowered his weapon as he glanced at Williams.

"*Ich ergebe mich*," said the man, and dropped his weapon. The horse became agitated when the gun hit the ground. "*Ich ergebe mich*," the Kraut repeated. I kept my pistol trained on him.

At that moment Williams fired two shots from behind the lancer, who, without time to respond, collapsed, and the startled horse ran toward the fields through the smoke.

"What did you do that for? The man had surrendered, goddammit. There are rules, Williams, rules!" I said to him.

The orderly shrugged. The war had been poised to end that very day . . . we would have become prisoners of war . . . the German would at first have been our prisoner, and later we would have handed ourselves over to the cavalry, to the infantry, to the artillery, to the air force, then the German marines . . . I would have been able to kiss that Big Bertha they had down the way, polish it carefully, cover it with a multi-colored blanket, warm it with my breath at night . . . but no, the German lay there with two holes in his chest . . . I touched him with my foot, good and dead, no two ways about it, Williams had been too hasty . . . The lieutenant colonel groaned.

"I can't feel my legs," he said. Then he shouted: "Remove me from here immediately! That's an order. Remove the car, you pigs, you idiots, you fools and invalids . . . Williams, I'm going to take you to the court martial, I'll have you shot for abandoning an officer, for disrespecting military authority! Prepare yourself, Williams, deliver your soul to your Creator . . . you and the Portuguese should enjoy what remains of your freedom . . . I'll be at your sides the moment they unload their weapons on you, you imbeciles, I'll make sure the new recruits are the ones to do it, do you hear me, Williams, the most useless men I can find, blind or cross-eyed, the ones who show up on the frontlines with no eyes and still a bit of down sprouting from their cheeks. First, they'll get you in the knees, then in the stomach . . . they're terrible shots . . . Ah, and me here, on French soil . . ."

Williams shoved his weapon in his pocket and we departed for headquarters, the lieutenant colonel squawked, I looked behind me, inching closer and closer, the Germans covered the landscape in smoke, the projectiles fell, we quickened our pace, were almost sprinting through the countryside among chunks of carrot, we abandoned the road, could still hear the lieutenant colonel's screams.

"Bastards, thugs, criminals! My legs . . . I can't feel my legs, I can't feel them, degenerates . . ."

We came across the German lancer's horse, a fearful chestnut beast, it was performing curvets with it ears flattened close on its head . . . it was very demure! Williams attempted to capture it over the course of a minute or maybe more, grabbed at its reins, woah-woah-woah-horsey, although without success, we continued on foot, the horse disappeared into the rising black smoke and faded away past the wreckage of our car, which, meanwhile, was jettisoned into the sky along with the lieutenant colonel, the result of a well-aimed enemy artillery, they soared upward accompanied by the carrots, reunited in a shower of root vegetables and human flesh, a soup du Great War, quite a delicacy, we continued jogging through the fields, our feet sinking into the soft earth, it wasn't raining but at times a slightly cutting breeze kicked up. We stopped for a while and Williams scrutinized the horizon. At that point, he had already cursed the king of England, the British Empire, Europe, the stupid lazy French, the Germans and their ridiculous Kaiser with his one arm that was shorter than the other, that monster, that one-armed savage, a lunatic, the emperor had to shove one hand in his pocket in order to hide his deficiency, typically during official dinners, and use his smaller hand to hold the fork . . . Had Williams noticed my lack of proportions? I had no way of knowing . . . I rarely ventured a breath that might be squandered with futilities, and, therefore, I picked up my march, one leg led the other into a trot and my companion followed me along the turnip fields; lying in the berms we attempted to avoid were a few rotting cadavers serving up a quite a banquet for the flies that buzzed around us and, lord!, an atrocious odor the wind spread about, it penetrated my nostrils, fingered my brain and my taste buds, I could feel the rot in my mouth. I

THE DEVASTATION OF SILENCE

was covered in dirt, my uniform was muddy, and yet we continued until we reached an abandoned corral, Williams squinted his eyes, at a distance the German artillery was having a break, Big Bertha rested for a moment, our artillery responded from the columns to the left, and the Englishman quickly began to wander, moving away then drawing near, he walked ceaselessly, treading on the earth, the manure, the hay . . . he kicked at a tumbleweed made largely of mortar . . . I couldn't see a single building on the property we were occupying, however there was a large hole in the middle of the field, a crater of considerable proportions that I approached with caution, I noticed immediately a few vertical beams that had been scorched, their outsides cracking . . . there had undoubtedly been a house there, Williams quickly launched into an avalanche of complaints, the man was simply incapable of keeping his mouth shut, not even the smell or the smoke could stop him from speaking, not there, not on French soil, no, never on French soil, I, on the other hand, had no opinions on French soil, didn't understand the British fixation with it, I had no idea what could have bestowed French soil with such undesirable characteristics, it certainly wasn't any better or worse than Flemish soil . . . drier perhaps . . . Williams continued his garbled chant and we began our march anew, I didn't know exactly how far we had strayed from headquarters, we crossed through some fields, my companion suggested taking the road and trying to reach the few British troops we had encountered during our drive, but the idea struck me as dangerous . . . the men were likely far off by now, if they hadn't already been killed by the Germans . . . and I was almost certain there would be more projectiles, which would no doubt be our undoing, no, it was preferable to continue through the fields . . . he agreed, and half an hour later of walking among turnip clumps and foliage we arrived, at last, at our lines, at the barbed wire, the deep trenches, leaving the fields behind to the mercy of the Germans. It didn't matter to me if they occupied them or not. The following day some general would decide it was necessary to retake those kilometers, repel the enemy's advances . . . one day more, one day less, it was all the same . . . they were agricultural fields, and, as such, would have to be reconquered, if they had been empty, barren fields perhaps we wouldn't have fought so hard for them, but they were agricultural fields, and agricultural fields must be occupied, blast craters and all, Williams was happy and he smiled, for a moment I felt the wind and I'm sure I smiled too, the breeze, even if slight, always had that tranquilizing effect on me, insofar as it made me recall indefinite hours spent observing humble and serene objects, the rare moments of satisfaction from my infancy; these days, I don't know quite what hold the breeze has on me. It's a mystery . . . In fact, it seems I don't smile much at all anymore. At least, not that I notice . . . I'm sure, however, that I don't possess that same tranquilizing presence the breeze does. I disturb those around me . . . the people I most adore . . . I infect them! Perhaps it has something to do with my asymmetry.

Upon cresting the final hill we noted burnt-up cars, an ambulance with no wheels, upturned dirt, and an unfinished ditch that extended for hundreds of meters. The torches were ablaze. Everything was calm. The night fell serenely over the tents, we descended the hillside, a British soldier driving a truck was doing circles and turns in a stretch of uprooted soil, having the time of this life . . . The guards ordered us to stop, although without much conviction, they recognized Williams, were from the same regiment, and welcomed him warmly, they didn't want to hear our story, they were hungry and had little to do . . . one of them was gnawing on a chunk of bread which was putting up quite a fight, but he didn't let up, from the way he chewed it I was sure he would have continued doing so even if his entire family had been murdered, he'd likely have kept on even as civilization itself collapsed, he feasted, and we carried on in pursuit of the major, whom we found in an illuminated tent, I was disheveled, my hair an utter mess, my mustache crooked, I'd lost my hat somewhere, my pants were covered in mud, it was, all in all, a lamentable state for a captain, an officer of the Portuguese Expeditionary Corps, and set a terrible example for my country, there was no denying it. I bent over to clean off the tips of my boots with my sleeve and combed my hair back with my fingers. At last, we entered the tent.

"Who's there? Announce yourselves, please."

Major Smith was seated at his desk, and, at his side, an orderly stood near the oil lamp, he was the one who questioned us, I noticed that the desk was very high quality, cherry, it appeared, and even had two small drawers . . . they certainly opened and closed! Likely without much noise! We introduced ourselves, saluted, Major Smith stared at us inquiringly, we began our report on the journey and described how we'd set out in search of the Portuguese command on account of the run-over chickens, and how the lieutenant colonel had been launched skyward.

"And what of the troops, Major?" I asked

"Troops? What troops? Oh, yes, of course. Well, we lost some men. And others were taken prisoner. But in any case, tomorrow we'll recapture our positions, two French battalions are on the way . . . on foot, you see . . ."

He took the fingers of his right hand on a stroll across the desktop, and I advised him that our current position was exposed to enemy forces, then watched as the major halted his fingers' march and began to drum them. The wood was of excellent quality, it had certainly been varnished.

"Listen here, we have been made aware, by a secure source, that the Krauts won't advance because they lack the men. They recruit children fresh off their first communion. Communion, my good sirs! Or younger. They might as well be snagging them from the baptismal font, out of their mothers' arms, plucked right from the bosom of the priest before their bath has ended . . ."

"But Major . . ."

"I've already told you, man, the information is reliable: we'll retake control of the positions tomorrow, without a doubt. As long as Fauchet . . . look, don't worry yourself with all this. Tell me, was it the lieutenant colonel who decided to take the car to look into the chickens?"

"Yes, Major," Williams responded.

"Who drove the vehicle?" Smith inquired.

"Me, Major," said Williams.

"Sit down, please."

The orderly offered Williams a chair, Major Smith also sat down, smoothed his mustache, rubbed his belly, and drummed his fingers once again on the desk, his other hand grabbing a piece of paper and a pen. He questioned Williams regarding the chickens following a moment of silence, these hens, these roosters, what species were they, how much did they weigh, what was the nature of their plumage? He was methodical.

"It must have been French poultry, then. What would you say their dimensions were, Williams? Did they seem to meet the standard proportions of the local species? Did they appear well fed?"

"In truth, I can't say."

"You can't say. Very well then."

The major scribbled on his paper. Afterward, he drafted a report utilizing all available data and rolled the tips of his mustache while scratching his stomach.

"I believe I have everything I need. I drafted the comments myself and will ensure this report reaches the Portuguese command. Jeffs," he turned to the orderly, "fetch Sergeant Clifford."

The orderly exited the tent and the aforementioned Sergeant Clifford appeared some minutes later, out of breath, and seated himself.

"Clifford, send this message to the Portuguese command," Williams said, and handed him the paper.

The sergeant went pale.

"But, Major, the Portuguese command is unreachable. The lines were cut during the German assault."

"What lines, Clifford?"

"The telegram lines."

"The telegram lines? Who said anything about telegram lines? Was it me?" He looked furiously at the sergeant, then, at Williams, turned his gaze to me, and ended with Jeffs, the orderly. "Was it me, Jeffs?"

"No, sir."

"Did I say anything about telegram lines?"

"No, sir."

"Are you sure?"

"I am sure, sir."

"Did I mention, perchance, sending a telegram?"

"No, Major."

"You're absolutely certain, Jeffs?"

"Absolutely, sir."

"Would you swear it on your mother's life?"

"My mother is already dead, sir."

"Yes . . . well, would you anyway?"

"Of course, sir."

Smith, triumphant, scanned the tent, the brown canvas, our faces, the shadows cast by the lamp, which stretched all the way to the dark rectangle at the entrance, then finally, he scratched his belly, and from his entrails rose a growl that halted in his closed mouth. He continued:

"Very well then, very well . . . what is required, Clifford, is prudence, extreme prudence . . . and care. Contain yourself, Sergeant." The man straightened himself and seemed, at the end of the effort, somehow smaller. "As I said, make sure this message reaches the commander of the Portuguese forces in the area. Choose a man, Clifford, don't send it by telegram."

"Sir, the Germans occupy the area that separates us from the Portuguese command."

"Yes, and . . . ?"

"Well . . . if I send a man to cross it, it's likely he'll be gunned down immediately, Major."

The major, irascible, slammed his fist down on his beautiful desk and replied:

"Being gunned down is what soldiers are for, Sergeant! Where is your patriotic spirit, Clifford?"

"Major, no . . ."

"Are you saying, then, that you believe a man shouldn't sacrifice himself in the name of the *sacra terra* . . . ?" The major stressed the Latin to the beat with which he slammed the desk again with his clenched fist.

He was eloquent, there was no doubt. I was, however, at that point, extremely hungry, that hunger that never again left me, my guts no longer stick to my bones, they don't cry out in pain but the discomfort is unceasing, I'm unable to eat without shame, I swallow my food in the blink of an eye, even today, it's true, and in that moment it was becoming increasingly difficult to listen to the major,

I hid a yawn behind my hand, Williams was growing impatient in his chair and rubbed his palms on his pants, Smith, once again drumming his fingers on his desk, concluded:

"Thusly, it behooves you to fulfill the function that the army and, above all, the British people demand of their sons. Remember: the desires of the people come to us from on high." And he handed the sergeant the document. "Send your best man. Or your second-best man."

Moments later:

"Matter of fact, send that red-headed short one, the one who looks like a dwarf, or a leprechaun; I get goosebumps every time I see him."

"Corporal Thompson?"

"How would I know, Sergeant? Do I look like I have the time to memorize the names of every man in the regiment?"

"No, sir."

It was impossible to think of everything, names, ranks, roles, it wasn't even easy to remember the names of all the weapons, gases, masks, gear, location designations, orientation points in the trenches, barracks, foreign officers, dates of provision deliveries, communications codes, rations passwords, attack and retreat commands, it was very complicated, and the soldiers didn't help, they were endlessly tiresome, incapable of following even the simplest wartime ground rules or codes of conduct, they didn't respect their superiors, didn't die when they were supposed to . . . that story about the hens was clearly eating Major Smith alive, corroding his liver, exploding like shrapnel in his belly, melting him down, and, as if that weren't enough, there were also the cockerels, the roosters, an investigation was clearly needed, it would be indispensable for preserving order . . . and Fauchet was either arriving or not arriving with the

Frenchmen, it was still unknown . . . Sergeant Clifford saluted him and ran from the tent with the envelope in hand. Smith was, indeed, a meticulous officer. Having returned to complete concentration on his desk, he stroked his mustache and sucked his teeth, asked us if we had already eaten, told us we looked faint, had the faces of men who needed a meal, had we forgotten to feed ourselves or take proper care of our needs, clearly we had been negligent and it didn't make for a pretty view, we were rotting at attention like old trees without ivy or moss to hide us, our naked trunks, it was utterly deplorable . . . How very uplifting! We gave him the appropriate salute and exited the tent, my stomach groaned, Williams, for his part, complained of a certain malaise, perhaps they had poisoned him . . . all typical of wartime, perfectly normal . . . The only thing left was for me to rejoin my company, get caught up on the news and, above all, eat something. We parted ways . . .

I noticed that so much time seated on the toilet had made my blood circulation poor and I abandoned the latrines as Williams glanced at me, the British gibbon had lost some hair as well as some weight, despite having his pockets filled . . . those endless pockets . . . a wealthy simian with a growing hair loss problem . . . how demoralizing! I almost asked him for a cigarette but opted not to speak.

Outside, the air was saturated with mist, a sticky white moisture, I shivered, it had chilled me and I decided to take a walk before returning to the barrack, a guard crossed my path, him and his ridiculous helmet, he smiled dishonestly, I continued with my head down and, after a few steps, gave a half turn, through the fence I saw some guards coming in from the forest, they advanced in pairs with a couple dogs in tow, they were doing the night rounds through the camp and had just finished with the cemetery, I remembered then that Slingshot had perhaps been buried that afternoon, he and the two Englishmen, someone had likely recited a beautiful eulogy and Slingshot, without a head, had no way of hearing it, the words abandoned to the porous earth . . . Where would his slingshot have ended up? I didn't know . . . The guards entered the camp, among them was a kind-looking youth, blessed with a natural gentleness, he certainly detested military service, and with good reason given the ridiculous hats they had to wear, between the Krauts' casserole lids and the Portuguese's sheep costumes, that war had pampered no one . . . our destiny was inescapable . . . and the gaiters, lord, the gaiters! . . . Following that, the soldier disappeared into the night, into the footsteps of his fellow Germans, and I departed.

Back in the barrack, I carefully opened the door and immediately overheard my companions' snoring and sneezing, and I spied Costa's feet, which remained visible even in the darkness. Upon crossing the room, one foot in front of the other, I realized I was starving, and I lay down and slept.

V.

My friend interrupted the waiter and requested two more teas to be served twenty minutes apart. The table was mired in porcelain, white shards lined in blue, handsome pastoral scenes, I had drunk my coffee long before, I too ordered a tea, he patted his coat, confirmed the tickets were still there, following which he adopted an irritated look, wanted to know once and for all if I remembered the day they recorded my voice, nothing beyond that interested him, I'd already told him that no, I hadn't forgotten what he'd asked of me, I remembered it in perfect detail, my memory is excellent, as long as you don't ask me the names of flowers, which are quite irrelevant in these modern times, this marvelous post-war era, frivolities . . . I know how to assemble and disassemble a machine gun, but what use do I have for flowers? Now, on the morning following Slingshot's death, we stood for *Appel* without incident, despite the rumors circulating that our allies had won a crucial victory in Flanders, the origins of such rumors were unknown, however the sound of planes had indeed been drawing nearer, and we had grown hopeful that someday soon the American tanks would arrive to liberate us. Timóteo celebrated to such an extent that he vomited, I don't know what the man had in his stomach that was worth vomiting but that is what happened. There is no such thing as an impossibility. He regurgitated a greenish-yellow phlegm, it must have been bile, gastric acids, perhaps he'd consumed some kind of herb . . . It wasn't unheard of that men would touch herbs to their lips, wild radish as well, snails, locusts, weevils, others tried chewing on bedbugs, sprinkling them on rinds rummaged up from the trash, it was an interminable battle and impossible to win, our beds were teeming with the tiny creatures, they had taken control of the barrack, had seized the war by its helm. If a general had ever awoken to find bedbugs in his living quarters, the war would have come screeching to a halt, ended that very instant . . . Paradise is a bed free of blood-sucking parasites, those creatures that keep us from carrying out our mission to spill our blood for God and country, to die for our homelands, or at least to lose an arm or leg for them—they rob us of our precious liquids, it is hell.

We stood there against the wall, groomed and in orderly, single-file rows, Schiller meandered among us, his cat in his arms, it would seem it had only run off for the day, and had returned with its fur all a mess, the Commander resolved to descend the platform in front of the Kommandantur and set about inspecting the men with a smile, their shaved and reddened heads beneath their caps, their irritated skin, the view pleased him, and yet, however satisfied he may have been, Schiller wasted no time in rattling off some incomprehensible phrases, he prattled, he prophesized, the minutes grew longer, felt more like hours, it grew hot, the tired guards watched him, and we, the prisoners, held ourselves up as best we could, until the first man fell, a Portuguese soldier . . . Schiller garbled his unceasing German . . . Then, it was a Russian, a human beanpole, a rod clanging to the floor . . . Schiller continued, he couldn't be restrained, his voice rose higher, shouting what it fell to him to announce, he forged ahead, I tried to concentrate on the words and learn some of what he was saying despite the hunger, my stomach was prodding the walls of my abdomen, it bounced up and down, left and right, it was very unsettling, nausea took hold of me, the acid drew near to my mouth, begged me for something to nibble on and Schiller, the bastard, walked to and fro with pomaded hair, his cat curled to his bosom, there was no way to shut him up, to clog his trap, man slips into madness and returns in a flash, the strength of it is staggering . . . I was swimming in subtle mental extravagancies, looping thoughts, I wished I had never been born, I cursed my parents yet again, the moment of conception, why had they given in to their lustful desires?, they'd only brought forth more misery, as if being born wasn't enough, that carnival of blood and excrement, a miserable situation, my head spun, I was consumed by dizziness, I resisted, withstood my penance stoically, others, however, lost consciousness, each row lost a few men to the ground, the sun was torturous, it joined in chorus with Schiller, that deviant, the June heat beat down on us, scalded our necks, left abrasions . . . Medical attention was needed, yes, it behooved me to strike up a conversation with Lang and his compresses, his gauze and surgical thread. At last, Schiller fell silent. Some twenty-odd prisoners threw themselves to the ground and we were freed from formation, everyone directed themselves quickly to the tent that served as a kitchen, a veritable pigsty, a stable, I wanted to accompany them, but mid-stride I was detained by Schiller and Müller, by the two of them plus another, a young new recruit.

"Follow us, *mein Herr*," ordered Schiller, but not without a certain kindness.

And so I did, we walked, entered the Kommandantur, scaled the stairs, those movements weren't easy for me, my kidneys hurt, I was experiencing explosive cramps, my innards whipped frenetically around inside me, they were clamoring for sustenance . . . That morning soup . . . I held my empty bowl in my hand, good lord, it seemed to have grown smaller, withered, it was dwindling before my very eyes, a dwarf bowl! Even if I had been standing before the kitchen my appetite couldn't have been sated by a dwarf bowl made for dwarf appetites . . . What a scandal, a prisoner of war with established rights, an officer, the situation sickened me. The tiny bowl mocked me, I stayed quiet, a closed mouth!, and ascended, my voraciousness propelled me, it was as if I were eating the wooden stairs, the splinters lodged themselves between my teeth and imprisoned themselves in my gums, I salivated.

Once we arrived in the room that served as an office, Schiller seated himself at his desk and I noticed immediately that, just about a meter and a half to one side of it, they had placed a long table and three chairs, another chair stood in front of Schiller and, across from that, a small table also accompanied by a chair, there was no shortage of chairs in that room, the Germans really gave it their all when it came to war, they were unstoppable, and, without unnecessary digressions, the commander requested that I sit, I hesitated and he urged me quickly to seat myself, he was suddenly quite worked up, indeed, he flew off the handle, he was distraught. If you can call a man distraught, you can likely also deem him hysterical, which is to say, he was hysterical.

"*Mein Herr*, sit, please, sit on the little . . . how do you say . . . the *Stuhl* . . . please."

He passed the cat off to a soldier while I remained standing, once again apprehensive because the chair appeared to me to be inordinately narrow, it was shrinking at the same rate as the bowl, an object I was unsure where to place.

"Commander Schiller, would you show me where I might place my dish?"

He rebuffed the question with a flailing of his arms, his wax-encased head hesitated, he was floundering beneath the portrait of Wilhelm II and urged me, again, to seat myself, to do him the favor . . . That overgrown, greased-up pig giving me orders . . . I obeyed. I sat, placed the bowl on the ground between my feet, I felt a chill, the room was penumbral, ideal for wretched, viscous, frog-like beings, moist-skinned lizards that, contrary to the laws of nature, don't seek out heat, the deviants.

"We will begin the hearing shortly," Schiller affirmed.

"What hearing, Commander?"

"Why, the hearing whose objective is to determine your role in the illicit activities that took place in barrack number 4, *mein Herr*, your role!"

My role, of course. I'd forgotten! I didn't respond, nothing occurred to me to say, I waited. Some moments later, Müller grumbled something, and Chaplain Howard and three soldiers—one of whom was Sergeant Bartz—entered the room, an orderly seated himself at the smallest table and procured a heap of papers and an inkwell, while

Bartz and a captain sat at the longer table; Howard claimed the third chair.

Schiller told me that, for my benefit, he would speak initially in French.

"It is for your convenience, so that you might better understand, that I will begin by speaking in French," Schiller told me. And further: "Despite not being required to, I will speak in French to aid in your comprehension."

I thanked him, and he continued.

"Ergo, my good sirs, ergo, we shall proceed as per the code of military conduct of the Imperial German Army with regard to this case. Note everything down, Kraus, don't omit a thing. Ah, this head of mine, you don't speak French, Kraus," and so he spoke to him in German.

Following that, he presented for judgement by the convocation the accused: a prisoner of the camp since last April, an individual who had recently submitted a request for change of interment location on the grounds of military rank . . . without documents, without documents!, and who, on the previous night, was caught in blatant disregard of the norms of this institution. As proof of my involvement, Sergeant Bartz would present to us in due course, the . . . the . . . what's the word in French?

They looked at one another, confused and surprised, then traded a few words in German, I confess I couldn't keep up . . . Frenzied, Schiller slammed his fist on the table, and with good reason, the commander's only request was to know what the French word for the object in question was, the safety pin, and nothing more!, he was modest enough in his pretentions, yet no one could answer him. I considered intervening, however, it seemed to me unreasonable to do so given my current position, I opened my mouth and promptly closed it. The discussion continued, and, suddenly, Schiller erupted:

"*Épingle! Épingle!*" he repeated, and was overcome by an exuberant happiness, everyone rejoiced, the secretary-orderly barely contained his applause, behind me Müller whispered, "*Eine Stecknadel!* Hmm . . . *Épingle!*"

Such was the Commander's war cry, seated at his desk, assailing it with punches and kicks, a desk with a scattered mess of papers on top, as well as brushes, paint tubes, pencils of various thicknesses, the artist had fused with the barrister, that was Schiller at that moment, a military man imbued with the creative spirit, claimed and lauded by the muses, in ecstasy. Meanwhile, my stomach was wreaking havoc on my back, it had pinned itself to my abdomen, which was riddled with malformations, contractions and distensions . . . No justice without food. They debated, Howard included, the latter stammering along in English, the session continued without incident, I have no idea what was said.

At that point Müller approached the long table and accepted the safety pin Bartz held out to him, he took it to Schiller, who examined it with all due attention, he lifted it to his eyes, the proof of the crime: illegal bets, games of chance, the barbarity in the prisoners' camp, the disrespect for civilization and mankind's transcendent values, the dereliction, the perversion, the rampant debauchery, the desecration, the horror. The crime had moved the Commander deeply, it would be impossible for him to treat the case with anything less than rigorous attention, it was understandable, even paramount, Schiller gesticulated and his papers scattered, a few sketches leapt off the desk and landed on the floor, the scribe rewetted the pen in the inkwell frequently, the soldiers concurred, Schiller was reason incarnate, he probed me:

"Tell me, *mein Herr*, do you have any objections? Do you deny the accusations?"

"No, sir."

"You don't deny having succumbed to the deceit of gambling?"

"No, sir, I don't deny anything."

"Is there anything you would like to add?"

"I would only add that what was wagered was a mere safety pin."

"A mere safety pin! The tool of corruption is irrelevant, as our friend the chaplain can attest, aware as he is of our troops' moral obligations. Isn't that right, Father?"

Howard babbled something unintelligible, which sounded to my ear like braying, it reminded me of the donkey that belonged to the olive-oil seller who used to stop by my house; the smell was similar too.

"It is useless to appeal to the singularity of the object, nay, I would say it is in fact reprehensible to rely on vile gimmicks, which could never deflect the illegalities you have involved yourself in, you, my good sir, and your accomplices."

I conceded. In truth, my head, which was much too light, was preventing me from forming any subtle or elevated thoughts, I glanced at my bowl . . . It continued to shrink, it was fading away and no one had anything to say about it! We were parasites, saprophytes, troublemakers, in Schiller's words, we undermined the foundations of a capable and dignified institution that welcomed everyone as children of its own, an entity, Schiller said, that held us in a familial embrace, as kin, and my accomplices and I had rejected it, we were the camp lice, ergo, the fleas, he bet we had tried to escape, might well have said we'd had a hand in everything, we spread rumors like pests, cholera, gossip regarding French planes, spectacular American victories, we had likely reintroduced tuberculosis to the prison population, we were outlaws, miscreants, scum, he raised a handkerchief to his forehead, it was hot in there, my silence was no surprise to him, not in the slightest, he also admired the fortitude with which I confronted this virtuous inquiry without resorting to biased chicanery, to hollow gestures aimed at less dignified ends, he forged ahead with a long list of accusations and adjectives, I allowed him to speak without interruption, in truth I'd say I hardly heard much more than that and whatever I heard was what I heard, it wouldn't have made a difference if he had been speaking in German . . . The hunger pained me deeply, my unsated appetite reprimanded me for the choices I'd made, my inability to make amends tortured me . . . why not try to get out of the sentence that hearing was soon to impose? Stupid games, Timóteo and Lopes and Costa and the other fools were all degenerates, they were filling their bellies right then with me here, seated beneath the lewd, lustful gaze of Wilhelm II and his gigantic mustache, perhaps a revolt unbeknownst to me had occurred, the informers had hunted me down, sold me for a plate of lentils, a heaping plate of them, I'd certainly give up something of value for some lentils, a finger, a pointer finger, a thumb, a toe, two toes, even a vertebra.

I restrained myself. The Commander rounded out his allegations entirely in French, he was generous in that respect:

"Therefore, and as you, my esteemed colleagues, will certainly come to understand, the most basic justice would be to issue punishment to the transgressor and, thereby, to hold this individual up as an example to future transgressors. Ergo, it is my opinion that the penalty for these crimes requires complete isolation and that, given his excellent physical form, the accused should have his rations reduced. As of tomorrow morning, a cell and reduced rations, my good sirs."

The beast! Excellent physical form, he said, and with this bodily asymmetry! Incredible, what insolence, how savage, and the proposal was, from the looks of it, accepted with good humor . . . Schiller didn't neglect to perform a subsequently pompous and rambling closing statement, veritably sopping with ceremony, the others applauded. I longed to eat, I wondered if they'd already taken away the soup pans, I acquiesced, accepted everything, he asked me if anything had occurred to me to say, no, nothing at all, the camp commander cautioned me of an uncertain future in another camp, he was soft, even docile, a lamb, that Schiller, even if I gave his claims no credence, he counseled that I would soon be convinced of their truth, suggested that I not assume an inflammatory attitude, that I curb my more intimate instincts, those antisocial impulses that sprung, to put it bluntly, from my horrifyingly weak character, I was a monster, ergo, an encourager of assassins not above the killing of harmless animals, cats for example; what place do cats have in war, I might have asked him, if he were to be so kind and elaborate?, I would personally have left them in peace, solitude, I was tired, apathetic, I remembered the scientists who were soon to arrive in the camp to record the prisoners' voices, the phonologists or musicologists, Lang's enthusiasm in sharing the news, I should have asked the lieutenant doctor to send the letter for me, as it was indeed in my pocket, it had crumpled in a horrifying manner, fallen victim to atrocious creasing and lost much of the purity of its pencil markings, asked him to send the letter and give me a cigarette, or a pack of them, but I had missed my opportunity, who would sing for the Germans?, someone would likely recite them a poem, but those bumpkins of mine were illiterates one and all, perhaps one of them—some sad sack—would lose his marbles spelling out some word he didn't know. The hearing ended, I was free for the rest of the day. They had been kind.

"*Mein Herr*," I glanced at Schiller's papers, "Commander, you wouldn't happen to have a portrait of . . ."

He tweaked his mustache rapidly.

"*Nein, nein.*"

And so I descended the stairs, followed by Müller. Outside, the sun was already high, and I came face to face with Le Bidon, who was waiting for Müller, they approached one another and seemed almost to embrace as they traded some object between them whose outline I couldn't discern, their brotherly affection moved me deeply, shortly thereafter Le Bidon pursued me.

"How'd things go?" he asked, breathless.

"Fine."

"Hmm," he went quiet. Afterward, he said, "They're saying you're being sent to work on the front, close to Armentières."

"Armentières? No, that's a lie."

"Well then?"

"Well, what?"

"Where are you going?!"

"To a cell."

We arrived at the kitchen and, of course, there was no food, I sensed I was collapsing, my body was five, six, seven centimeters below my mind, my ideas hung buoyant above my head, the unconsciousness lasted mere seconds, following which I forced myself to accompany my body closer to the earth.

"Hungry, old man?" Le Bidon inquired. "No friend of Le Bidon's gets sick while I'm around . . . No, sir!"

I made an effort to glance at the Frenchman, albeit without success, as my head was spinning.

"Let's go."

And so we went, me beside Le Bidon, my bowl in my hand, the light dazzled me and he babbled incessantly, he was my friend, he affirmed, my brother, and I could do him a favor, an act of goodwill between friends. I assented as I lifted biscuits to my mouth, they were a bit moist but even so I ate them, I felt bewildered, my vision was not infrequently cloudy, the pressure pummeled my cranium, my thoughts slipped away in the same instant as they arose, all in the name of *la mère patrie*, Le Bidon explained, another man horny for the homeland, they were too numerous to count in those days, infected by some airborne ailment, some waterborne illness, or perhaps it spread through the exchange of bodily fluids and humors, yes, everything we did was a test of our love for the motherland and the dear ones we had left there, didn't I have a wife, what was that pale mark circling my finger, its significance was probed, he was curious, meddling, men who thrive in prison always are, the rats! . . . By god! I didn't respond to him, I ate more biscuits, the ones he kept stored in his pocket, the same pocket out of which he then procured a small paper package, I had only to deliver it to Lang, he had noticed we were friends, deliver it to him before being locked in my cell, if that was really the case. If it was the case! Schiller had decreed it without fear or favor due to the crime in question, and to preclude any putrefaction of the soul that might occur from contact with the monster, it was a question of camp hygiene, cleanliness was indeed next to godliness! We were in agreement.

Some minutes passed and Le Bidon remained faithfully at my side. We were seated, the day continued calmly and without interruption, a northern wind had kicked up, it was refreshing, did me good, it was warm out, I stretched my legs and leaned back against the wall of the tent where he slept.

"Did you stash the package?" he asked.

"Yes," I said.

"Where?"

"Doesn't matter."

"Don't lose it . . . for the love of *la mère patrie* . . ." he parroted.

"Be quiet," I told him.

I wanted to hear a robin crooning its melodious song, but Le Bidon wouldn't shut up, he was like a mortar launcher, at last the robin's song graced my ears, the Frenchman stood before me still, my vision reacquired a certain acuity and he appeared to me in all his foulness, he was a disgusting toad with those sloping cheeks that mocked our starvation, he stuffed himself during times of scarcity, he was radiant, had been fortifying himself, just another human tick, Schiller was slacking on his cleanup duties . . .

"We are, however, in agreement?" he hesitated.

"Yes, yes, but be quiet."

Delivering the package didn't perturb me, I had no issue hiding things in my boots, or even my mouth for that matter, armpits or groin, it was all the same to me, I only cared that he be silent. In that moment, I thought I also heard a blackbird.

My friend in the café asked me if that was the day they'd recorded my voice, which was, in fact, the only topic he was interested in, I only want to know about the day your voice was recorded, he said, I don't care about anything else besides the story of how they recorded your voice, nothing you're telling me is at all important, he said and admitted, I even find it somewhat inappropriate, tell me how they recorded your voice, it's the only story that has garnered my interest. I asked that he be patient, suggested he have a sip of tea, he was mercurial, much different from my companions. The barrack was calm that night.

"Th . . . th . . . they say the Americans are on the way, m . . . my . . . my ca . . . captain," Fonseca stuttered. "And . . . and . . . that . . . that . . . the French planes . . ."

I didn't listen to the rest, I set myself to observing the barrack, the young Lopes seemed melancholy, likely an aftereffect of dinner, which had consisted of potato soup with nettles and beet skins, water really, water and nothing more, his emotional state was understandable and, furthermore, he'd been sick lately, his flushed expressions indicated a fever, a condition that had ailed him for days . . . Words were shared in confidence, I ignored the general observations, Fonseca's rehashed and superficial conversation, that one certainly wasn't perturbed by the dark possibilities of a new imprisonment location, excessive work, I had already seen men go crazy from work, as the Russian in the infirmary could attest, the cripple who'd shoved his hand under the train car . . . If a man has enough to eat, work can be bearable, however, the heartlessness of labor is grotesque, labor is a natural aberration, or better put, a human aberration, my father was right on the money when he said labor makes a brute of a man . . . What did Fonseca know? Would they still take him to the German scientists, the phonologists, to recite a beautiful poem, even with that stutter of his? It was possible. Lopes certainly wasn't a stutterer, that much was true, he carried on at length regarding his past, grew deeply in touch with his inner poet, was consumed by thoughts of his lamb, he brought it up again, his mother needed money, to him the sheep was a part of the family, but Lopes had been sent off, what could he do? At its core, it all boiled down to a trap a woman had set in his path, that wartime classic: if it wasn't the country's fault, it was the fault of some woman, or various women, the men were always innocent, of course, it's always due to someone else, a fascinating factoid to be listed along with the tidbit that the snapper had invented labor, that crime can be blamed on wolves, and hunger on rats, Lopes was certain his name had been suggested to the recruiters by a woman he'd rejected, an old widow without a bloodline, she had courted him, called to him from below his window, he was in love with another woman, his Mariana, didn't have eyes for some bitty, for which reason she had used her influence to spitefully have him called up for duty, his cousin remained there in the village and he in France, ah, life was cruel . . . I asked him if the widow possessed sufficient power and connections within the Ministry of War and Lopes was sure of it.

"She's the one to blame!"

That belief nurtured him and he rose up excitedly onto his elbows, he was unhinged, consumed by pure madness! It was something one could grab hold of, much better than stale crusts, but Lopes had gone completely gaga. Someone then suggested a game of dice for a cigarette, I refused, and Lopes rolled over on his pallet bed, he wasn't in the mood to gamble.

"Can you tell us about Papua, my captain?"

And why not? I began telling them of the verdant forests, the rivers, Lopes grew very excited, you might well have said he was close to shoving off and having it out with every Kraut along the way, another sign of madness, fever, he was hallucinating . . . I had no choice but to calm him down, no easy task, and I returned to Papua's natural features.

"Marvelous. How do you know so much about Papua, my captain?" he asked.

I shrugged, I knew and that was enough . . . better to keep my mouth shut! Some theatrics here and there but nothing more, after all, one must put on a show! As it was far too hot on my pallet bed I decided to take in some fresh air, leave the pestilent odors of the barrack behind, it certainly didn't smell of open stomachs, spilled guts, yet I felt I was suffocating, I exited, Dr. Lang was also passing through, hands clasped behind him, he recognized me immediately, stopped me in my tracks, we began walking together, he was fleeing the humors of the infirmary, the stench, he too had grown intimate with the fragrance of fear, sweat mixed with vomit and excrement, it is indeed one of the fundamental odors of our species, he guaranteed me, the other, he had concluded throughout this long career, was that of mothers' milk, hot diapers, mended baby clothes, such were the odors and they screamed for their mothers, but why?, perhaps they cried out at the end the same as they had in the beginning, in order to close the cycle of shame their scandalous birth began, there's no rational justification, they'll never again taste their mother's milk, and yet they wax nostalgic about childhood even though she is precisely the one who brought them into this life of suffering, it was entirely senseless . . . The idea had tormented him ever since my visit to the infirmary, he had begun to notice how they cried for their mothers, among other things. I could believe it if I wanted, it was his honorable word and nothing more, but the fact is that one of the men had cried out for his dog who had been run over by a carriage many years prior, it had been pulled under the wheel, he remembered it now, his little dog, the beast would lovingly lap at his face and the Australian—he was an Australian—now lie there inert, covered in pus, he was one big pustule, certainly no one there would touch him willingly, but the dog, oh yes, the dog would have, and he cried out for *Tobby . . . Tobby, Tobby!* . . . Tobby was long gone, the Australian lay stretched out, it was quite shameful, patients conjuring up memories of people who had nothing to do with war, they should have been more discerning, bringing up dogs during wartime, have you ever . . . Schiller had raised the same question regarding cats. The Germans are dedicated ponderers, they spotlight extremely curious conundrums, one would never reach a comparable civilizational milestone from our cliffs and gullies . . . And the mothers! What reason would a mother have to bear witness to the death of her child? Perhaps she could hold the entrails in her hat? The mother was Dr.

Lang, him and his morphine, whenever he procured it, Lang was God, of course, he saved them from death regardless of their place of origin or religion, he could cure anything a little bit, except for baldness, which, to be honest, was an area in which he found himself far from savoring the taste of success, countless men had sought him out, both covertly and conspicuously, they consulted him regarding the possibility of a voluminous tuft, he didn't withhold it from them, however it had already caused quite a few squabbles, even commander Schiller had requested his help, who would have thought, what with that lustrous coiffure, I shouldn't let myself be fooled, however, all one had to do was note attentively the rug's excessively dark color, Lang insisted on convincing me that Schiller suffered from hidden baldness, he wouldn't let me leave, we walked in circles, Lang had given me his arm like an old friend, I, on the other hand, hadn't dined with the same abundance as he and quickly grew dizzy, I cursed the doctor, his blond hair and his entire family, I wished, once again, that they all rot in hell, that he and his relatives be blown to bits, shredded to pieces, the horse was the only innocent among them, Lang's pig of a father-in-law could roll his tobacco with his daughter's skin folds, he could cut them from her corpse, perhaps get a whiff of the odor of war, maybe he'd even soil himself while he was at it, Lang was deeply concerned by contagious diseases, certain dermatological blights in particular made him cringe, his wife told him he was aging prematurely with worry, but the truth is that those illnesses were transmitted through touch, somewhat like those so-feared plagues of the past, whose causes appeared supernatural even, sometimes all that was needed was an exchange of objects for contagion to spread, I acquiesced and mumbled that yes, he was right, of course.

"Speaking of which, how are the new boots?" he asked, he wanted to know how my new boots were treating me, I glanced at the boots I had recently acquired, the ones I'd taken from Slingshot, I'd settled into them well, I had no reason to deceive him, they fit me perfectly, which is exactly what I told him, they fit me perfectly, I feel good in these boots, they are, in fact, excellent boots. We then changed topics, Lang rejoiced at the imminent arrival of the phonologists, he hadn't been able to sleep from anticipation, the following morning I would be trapped in isolation, due to which I yearned to get on with the goodbye as quickly as possible, the doctor's words were torture, my desire was to order him to shut up, but I found myself unable to do so, he stalled, he dwelled, his anticipation transformed into profound emotion, his wife had been deceiving him with the farmer next door, he sobbed, the one he bought the horse's oats from, upon discovering her infidelity the previous night, Lang had threatened to kill the horse as revenge, his wife had called him gutless, a sorry excuse for a man, the doctor felt belittled and, naturally, had grabbed his saber, he was on the brink of splitting his wife down the middle when he remembered his children, those innocents, if they were indeed his!, and the war effort—more than anything, the war effort. He wouldn't deliver himself to prison, take the easy way out, far from it, he had to atone for his sins through action, yes, through the fever-pitch of war, he would request a transfer to the frontlines immediately, wherever they might be, in France, Flanders, the West, it made no difference to him, let them send him to Africa where he could drown his wounds, it occurred to me to suggest Papua New Guinea, however I contained myself, I wasn't sure what it might give rise to. A closed mouth! My decision soon proved itself correct, given that Lang's farmer neighbor was a Dutchman, who's to say he didn't have a cousin in Batavia, for example, the proximity became painful, one draws certain parallels because of it, Lang's problems were numerous, this gentleman didn't want to vent simply on a whim, no, he had suffered atrociously, his wife was, to top it off, a deviant, she had a habit of stealing clothing and fabric from stores and seamstresses, pieces belonging to other clients as they awaited their final proofs, reams upon reams of unsewn fabric, raw material fresh off the loom, it was a scandal, to put it bluntly, his father-in-law had fled Hamburg out of shame, had initially been able to handle the embarrassment and tried to buy off the police with tobacco, cigars of the highest quality, but the commissioner wasn't a fan of smoking, what a shame, and didn't appreciate his attitude, wasn't kind, nothing of leniency, an affront against commerce was a capital offence in the city of Hamburg, the thefts had shocked the populace, accustomed as they were to a righteous Hanseatic tradition, legal proceedings were initiated and picked up steam, grew relentless, bulldozed everything in their path including the good name of the family patriarch and his business, these were the conditions under which Lang had accepted his future wife, it was the purest of truths. He was aware of her proclivities and debts! A lunatic . . . Love drove him to act with compassion without thinking of his career, he moved far from any city, away from a promising future in Berlin or in Paris alongside the great figures of Science, and away from Dr. Leclerc-Armand, now all he has left is his wife who betrayed him, what's more with a good-for-nothing Dutchman with dirty fingernails, encrusted, slovenly, what a bunch of swine, Lang sewing up wounds while his lascivious wife rolled in the hay with some greasy nobody . . . And the children! He was an honorable man, were he not he would call into question his responsibilities regarding the offspring . . . the true paternity of the children . . . at least the horse was his, he'd have good reason not to lend it to his neighbor for tilling that year, he could plow the fields himself, pull the plow with his teeth, and Lang's bruiser of a wife could serve as the weight atop the machine, the furrows that year would be good and deep.

By the looks of it Lang had no shortage of saliva, the patrols crossed paths with us as he prattled on, but Lang, absorbed as he was, didn't even acknowledge their greetings, those twists and turns and the concentration required demanded efforts far greater than what remained to me, given that dinner had long since been digested, but I didn't rebuff Lang, the German remained a glowing confidante, the lieutenant-doctor wouldn't have carried on in the same way with a compatriot, a brother-in-arms, I was a sympathetic man, a compassionate enemy, I could count on him even if I was an asymmetrical monster. As much as he had tried, he couldn't forget his wife's betrayal, after all, he'd caught her on her back, had given in to animal instincts, the memories ate away at him, he told me he'd rather see himself in the trenches . . . he'd never felt a bullet in his body, or shrapnel, but he'd have no problem fighting among the tanks, advancing with a weapon in hand, he had renounced his position as officer and his functions as a military doctor, he'd been imbued with life . . . The treachery!

"Hear this, my dear, the man hardly even knows how to talk, and she thought herself so cultured that only French speakers would satisfy her! Well, well, by the looks of it she deluded herself. He smells of the stable, you know. His hands are calloused, what pleasure could there possibly be in his touch?" I didn't know and he continued: "Have you seen my hands? Look at them here . . . And I have options. I could give in to vagrancy, start frequenting brothels. A medical officer, someone in my position . . . Pah! Women would fall at my feet, they would throw themselves to the floor in my honor, supplicate themselves for a single caress, a wink, I guarantee you it is the purest of truths, my dear. And the Red Cross volunteers with whom I've crossed paths over the course of the war? Do they seem like throwaway women to you? Well not to me they don't, my wife is no goddess, I assure you of that, she's getting noticeably fatter, her paunch is growing and she's also acquiring a sort of dewlap, the children make fun of her, ask her if she stores her coin purse in there. Ah, those little rascals are funny, for her I won't lift another finger . . . and to think I exiled myself to the countryside for her . . . but there's nothing I wouldn't do for them. You understand, my dear, you're likely also a family man . . ."

My legs faltered beneath me, I forced myself to continue, Lang then offered me a cigarette and I accepted.

"For the children I weather all life's hardships, you see, they're my angels." I was frail, I almost tripped and yet I lugged along beside him. "Well, well, my dear, but tomorrow we'll have our scientists, how marvelous, spectacular even, such a shame about these dermatological illnesses . . ."

Lang's insistent words might have provoked unexpected reactions from me, yes, more words perhaps . . . in any case, I began to experience a certain itching on my arms, on my legs, my forehead and face, even my nose . . . In the dark, the doctor didn't notice how I scratched myself, just a little at a time, I exercised restraint, held back my question, remained silent, by God, the situation was coming together in a most disagreeable way, my nails tousled my tegument, gads, it was only making it worse, I'd thought of something concrete, however I no longer knew what, it was the soup's fault, it had been much too thin, the stalks had formed a ring in the pot and plopped with a splash into our bowls, the Krauts were killing us slowly through hunger and their incessant chatter, there was no escape, and Lang wouldn't shut up.

"Now when I go out in the street they smile at me disdainfully. And mind you, I just keep pedaling, I don't make a single deviation, even though I could make use of my position, but no, I go straight home and the she-devil's there rolling around with someone else, baking him cakes, that's why she was always asking me for eggs, now listen, eggs at a time like this, who does she think I am, a thief, a poultry poacher?! And all for what? They laugh at me, I tell you, I see them mocking me, they nicknamed me Cuckold, The Big Cuckold, Dr. Lieutenant Cuckold! And if they invite me over to someone's house, what will I do? Tell me, please, you're sensible, you don't speak just to hear yourself talk, you're thoughtful."

He stared at me plaintively, I scratched myself.

"Hmmm . . ."

"Ah, you can say it right to my face, I can take it. But I see you're much too cultured for that, you refrain from attributing the terms to me that I deserve: the dupe, the bumpkin, the pushover . . . But don't hold back, my friend! With me you can do as you please, in me you have a confidante, a supporter. Go on, tell me I'm a cuckold and an idiot!" he insisted.

In fact, I was unsure whether or not to respond; out of habit, I opt for the latter, as I'd already confessed to my friend and his teacups multiple times, in the long run it is the choice that yields the fewest problems, it is better to maintain ambiguity, uncertainty, it is a technique I've used throughout my life to enormous success, without it perhaps I would have never been made captain, I had perfected it during the war, its technical aspects as much as its linguistic functions, the words of our leaders rang true indeed when they claimed that war would usher its respective populations to their ultimate civilizational stage; on my part, my knowledge had only grown exponentially, there had been no down sides in fact, without even speaking of the practical skills gained, shooting mortars, for example, or using a bayonet or a mask, a few more years and we'd have developed gills and fins, yes, silence was invariably the best option. I stayed quiet.

Following that, Lang:

"I think of speaking with Howard. At the end of the day he's a man of God, his British principles are beneficial and stimulating."

I agreed, it was a great decision, despite the fact that I would have agreed with whatever he'd said at that moment, as all I wanted was to scratch and scratch, I passed my fingers along my legs, a low wind crept up along the ground and refreshed my feet, I had the desire to take off my shoes, Slingshot's boots felt tight, were cutting off my circulation, I felt an intense itchiness, veins that scaled my legs like pests, likely ticks, fleas, the depilation, oh, such torture, Lang always cogitating about something, it was late, the camp smugglers prowled the latrines, there was Bidon, Williams, the Russian with the limp, Müller, the guard who never requested time off, he was in the camp so often that by the end of the war he'd be rich as a badger; greed never rests however, and the man was visibly drained, it was impossible not to notice he hadn't slept in four years, he shed mustache hairs across the entire camp, perhaps they banded together with the cat hair, balls and balls of hair and fur, another hardship to withstand, Müller never stopped working, for which reason he accumulated money, he and the rest were erecting pyramids of gold. I scratched myself, it was an occupation like any other, respectable, Lang wasn't aware of my detainment in isolation the following day, because he continued to insinuate that I would be presenting myself to the commission of scientists, he was excited, he would finally find himself among his peers, life in the camp would no longer amount to curing tuberculosis, the commission was a shining light in his otherwise dull existence . . .

"As a soldier, there's nothing to stop me from exploding my neighbor's head, you see, as part of the war effort. War is war. The fellow isn't even really German, who can guarantee he's not sleeping with my wife for information? Military secrets, scientific theories, yes, yes, there are numerous attractions, of course, it's evident, he perhaps doesn't even desire her in physical terms, purely physical . . . the weight she's put on is hard on the eyes . . . and that she's lost in the face, despite her dewlap. She's not an appealing woman, to put it bluntly she's even somewhat repugnant. Those nails of hers, shoved coarsely into their beds. Little cow hooves! Nightmarish. She thinks she can run off with the Dutchman and leave the cuckold behind, yes, that's what goes through her head, and I'll have you know, my friend, that she spends her time daydreaming of canal rides on little boats, complete with a set table and a vase of flowers . . . Believes I'll raise the children for her . . . all the while, she's given herself over to debauchery . . . hedonism . . . We'll see about that."

The itching tormented me and the fatigue took hold; such is the misery of war. I remembered Lopes's observation, that it was preferable to die by projectile or bullet than to wither away in a bed like Almeida, from some vulgar illness, nothing militaristic . . . The boy was right, his concerns were relevant, as were those about the sheep and his advice to his mother . . . I still had the letter in my pocket, along with the other, it was there in my pants, of course, I moved my hand to it.

"Dr. Lang . . ." I said, and he, expectant, stared at me, I asked him if he could intern me in the infirmary, in order that I not be put into solitary.

"Perhaps," he said. "It's possible. But bedsheets are so expensive . . ."

Bedsheets were expensive . . . of course! There was no fabric, it had all ripped! And the contraband . . . I moved my hand to my pocket, where I had a secret stitched into the inside of my pants with a bit of fabric someone had likely torn from a bedsheet, I removed my wedding ring and extended it to him. Lang observed it and, a moment later, took it.

"Tomorrow morning, come by the infirmary," he said.

I was anxious to return to the barrack and sleep, I tried not to think of the itching, which was waning, all I had to do was return to my pallet bed, sleep is the final escape, and, deep down, there my yokels awaited me. The sky was clear, a sunny morning was all but guaranteed. If Lang would at least be quiet, everything would be easier.

VI.

I cleared my throat and my friend offered me another cigarette which I stored in my pocket; he asked me if, when everything was said and done, they had or had not recorded my voice, he only wanted to know if they had, if my voice had been documented by some machine, the rest interested him somewhat, but what he really wanted to know was if my voice was stored on a disk somewhere in Germany. The other stories might pique my interest, however, none so much as that of the recording, he told me, as he ordered two more teas because the previous two were cold, he had again forgotten to drink them. The waiter asked if we would be having lunch, if he should set the table for a meal, he replied to him that yes, we would be dining an hour from then, even though my stomach was already grumbling, the waiter departed for the service area, then the woman with the flowers entered the café and tried to sell me a yellow bouquet, they weren't white, I didn't buy any, she immediately caused a scene, insinuated that I was a tight-wad, a mere insinuation, however, as she didn't turn to me nor did she blurt the insult right out, but merely broadcast aloud that certain gentlemen thought themselves better than the rest for the simple fact of being seated at a café table, gentlemen who likely didn't even have any food to eat at home and who made the rounds of different establishments purely out of snobbishness . . . she wouldn't shut up! The waiter appeared with the first pot of tea, was unable to find a place for it on the table, the teapots had accumulated, my friend had been tapping his cigarettes into the cold liquid, the ashes floated in the yellow stuff, the flower peddler prattled on, flapped her arms, the waiter gawked, most certainly he thought himself the target of her many curses, I remained quiet as did my friend, the waiter grew furious and followed after her, left the café in order to argue with the woman, they began shouting in the street, I yearned to return to the conversation at hand, to enlighten my friend, he was anxious to hear me speak about the recording carried out by the studious Germans, the subject that most piqued his interest. My voice was recorded thanks to Lang's intervention, the doctor had kept his promise and I wasn't transferred to an isolation cell the next day, as he needed me nearby; he wanted to study me. I conversed over the course of approximately two hours with Schiller, he said, the Portuguese captain has a rare disease of the vocal cords, he'd assured him, I need the Portuguese captain in the infirmary because he has a rare disease of the vocal cords and could infect the other prisoners, he confirmed, if I don't intern the Portuguese for observation, he'd told him, we may well have an epidemic of this disease of the vocal cords, but if the Commander allows it, I'll intern him immediately and solicit the help of my colleagues from the scientific commission later on, as what we have here is a rare case of a disease of the vocal cords, he said. He convinced him. On top of that, he intended to introduce me to his wife.

Thus, early that morning and soon after formations, Lang and a soldier took me to the infirmary, where I installed myself and hid my bowl beneath a very scratchy pillow, the smell of which alone was enough to keep any curious parties at bay, it was a rank odor, the musk of various bodies, afterward I lay down on a bed with no sheets, however everything was much more comfortable than my pallet bed back in the barrack, Schiller would never enter the infirmary with that stench, however we had agreed I would fake being sick, racked with fever, aphonic. I wasted no time in contorting in my bed, Lang whispered that my portrayal was good, very good, the representation was excellent, I was a natural actor, upon lowering himself he offered me a cigarette, stuffed it in my coat pocket, smiled, and departed, I continued contorting for some time, and cried out. At my side, a Frenchman lifted his head, stared at me, and then lowered it back again, he also had on a threadbare infantryman's coat, he seemed agitated while he slept, his right leg didn't look well, appeared to have some kind of gangrene, a purulence, it likely needed to be amputated, he was only delaying the inevitable. I noticed, then, that, without realizing what I was doing, I had begun making an oscillating motion with my index and middle fingers, the two digits together forming a saw with which I was cutting the Frenchman's leg off in an imaginary fashion. I was nothing if not an esthete, my horror was at seeing so much pus, it wasn't pretty, I'm a simple lover of beauty, I've never been anything more than an appreciator of aesthetics, never sought anything more from my profession, that leg to me was an unfinished bridge, a fallen building, a hobbled cathedral, I was an esthete in the most refined and ethereal sense of the word, completely unable to take action, observation was the surest course . . . The Frenchman awoke bewildered, groaned, had no sense of the visual shock his leg provoked, bellowed—a horrible cry—no one ran to his aid and he went quiet.

As I found myself alone in the company of the infirm and wounded, I decided to get up and have a walk around the room, the space had nice windows, there was no shortage of light, the patients could read letters, newspapers, some didn't read anything because their eyes were covered in gauze, dressings of every kind, blood-stained and yellowed with pus, other patients lacked arms or hands, or they had them swaddled, all plastered up, on top of which it didn't smell particularly good, more than anything there was a man with the remains of a brown blanket covering his torso and a head that looked an awful lot like creamed spinach, quite a displeasing scenario, I kept my mouth closed as I hopped on tiptoe to avoid wrists, noses, and knees . . . I was lucky to have arranged a bed, Lang had proven himself obliging. If Lang provided me that luxurious cot he certainly wanted something else from me, I thought; however, we often judge people poorly, in truth, we don't always interpret them correctly, we almost never judge them objectively, I reflected, it is common for us to be unfair in our evaluations, as deep down, we're always unjust with others whether we know them or not, that is what occurred to me, that we hold preconceptions of those we don't know and grudges against those we do know or think we know, we are vesicles full of bile and bitterness for the people we've met, despite the fact we don't really know anyone; Lang is, along with all other people, more complex than is immediately obvious, I thought, perhaps he only pretends to help me because he likes me, despite us not really knowing each other, as is habitual when faced with someone with whom I don't share intimacy, I didn't trust Lang, our relationship was marred by suspicion, however, I concluded that I couldn't be sure Lang wanted me close by only for his own benefit. The doctor was consumed by his curiosity to hear me speak and sing in Portuguese, the satisfaction of hearing him speak of his wife, however, wasn't sufficient to convince me he didn't want to cut off one of my feet, or a hand, or an ear, perhaps my nose . . . Lost in digressions, I crossed the infirmary, there weren't many rooms, from the majority of them seeped the rancid fragrance of disinfectant and putrefaction, the rooms where the amputees were piled, few were the patients who didn't walk with some sort of aid, one was the Russian who had placed his hand on the train tracks, he was in the hall and waved to me from the shadows, I drew near to him and offered him a cigarette, he accepted it with his remaining hand, the other was a gauze-wrapped stump, and looked quite poorly, yellowed!, greenish-red in sections, it's possible that much of the rancid fragrance surrounding us and prickling our nostrils came from that rot, the putrescence spreading outward from the forearm, he had a match and lit his cigarette, wanted to offer me a light but I refused, didn't smoke mine, the nurses were nowhere to be found and Lang had disappeared, the morning gloom made the hallway melancholy, it was too early for the sun to strike the roof or the south-facing walls, the Russian didn't say anything, only nodded his head as if I'd asked him a question, I reciprocated with a similar gesture, he had also learned that the best demeanor is one of silence, a closed mouth, with my deformity and his stump we would be the perfect scapegoats, any problem that arose in the prisoners' camp would surely be caused by us, all the blame would be ours, even the war itself will have broken out on our account, the cripple and the amputee are always at fault, the two in the hallway concocting schemes and fantastical plans, we'd taken the war from the trenches to the underground, sunk the airplanes to the bottom of the ocean, we were perverts, mutants, the specialists wouldn't hesitate to ascribe us internal mirrors, correlate mental perversions with our physical deficiencies, or, perhaps, it would be that our mental deficiencies provoked our physical ones . . . a dilemma. I took my leave, went farther down the corridor, to my right were the rooms for bandaged heads, craniums completely wrapped in casts, rooms in which no seeing or hearing occurred, I noticed a nurse with unusual elbows. My God! His gown was stained around the chest, a bloodstain he surely hadn't washed as a water saving measure, he asked me what I was doing there, I understood that much, my German was improving from one day to the next, it was truly a marvel, a miracle of understanding, but I shrugged my shoulders, didn't feel like responding, didn't respond, he wanted to accompany me to my room, I followed him, there was little more I could do, I was pulled forward by those unfathomable elbows, they were in fact enormous, the nurse wasn't very tall, he only came up to my shoulder at best, the crown of his head didn't reach my neck, and yet his elbows spanned two men my size, me and the Russian, or me and Lopes and, perhaps, me and Lang and . . . Between sliced wrists and shattered ankles we arrived at the room where I had been interned, the moans increased as soon the nurse came into view, an Englishman complained of a swollen knee, the nurse stopped to examine it, but ended up wounding the man further with his misshapen arms, the Englishman howled, sent the room into an uproar, Lang emerged from the doorway and tried to calm the patients, the Englishman quieted, the nurse ran toward some distant cries arising from another room, almost trampled a few prisoners seated on the ground, I felt dizzy, what more could be expected of a person who hadn't eaten all day, I thought perhaps the dizziness was due to the smell of disinfectant and putrefaction, Lang ordered me to lay in the bed, it would behoove you to stay in bed, as if you were in fact ill, Lang whispered to me, if you run all over the infirmary instead of lying in bed, it will be hard to pass you off as infirm, Lang murmured, if Schiller were to do a surprise inspection, Lang said into my ear, he'd see you hopping around the infirmary instead of resting. What the doctor whispered made all the sense in the world, I thought, I didn't know how it hadn't occurred to me earlier, the hunger had made me that way, empty-headed, eager to lie down and sleep, I didn't think, but wandered instead.

Once I was lying down in my bed, Lang kneeled next to me and asked that I say a word in German. I didn't know what to say, which is why he asked me to say *Geschichte* and I did, I didn't mind, so long as he didn't require me to speak of Papua New Guinea, as my compatriots did . . . What fun, he laughed, begged me to say it two, three times, asked kindly and rejoiced, was overcome by giggles until he cried, his face contorted, I was his escape from his problems, lifted him above those arm stumps and acrid legs . . . The Germans knew how to enjoy themselves, they're a rigorous people, but, my, they do have a good time, and without lofty demands, Lang enjoyed my accent, say it again . . . oh, oh, oh, he cried, each is entitled to his small perversions, the committee of phonologists and other specialists wouldn't be long in arriving, Lang would present me to them immediately, would make a point to have me seen before the others, quite an honor, and with that German pronunciation of mine there was no question, I would dazzle them.

"Yes, it's impossible to not be delighted by you," Lang said, "there's no way they won't be ensnared by your charm, they'll be enchanted, I'm sure," he affirmed.

Lang's wheezing and whispering lulled me, I closed my eyes, too weak to push beyond the fatigue. I fell asleep, however, the malaise caused by my hunger disturbed me and I soon awoke, I looked around without lifting my head, I was starving and yet too tired to move, I yearned to recuperate my energy without the presence of food, at times hunger made the act of eating unbearable, unthinkable, repulsive, chewing was tiresome and, at the same time, essential, life's singular purpose. I wouldn't have found myself in that situation if I'd had the documents proving my military rank with me, I thought, if I hadn't lost my uniform and captain's insignias I wouldn't be here, where even the thought of food tires me, if they recognized my rank I would be in an officers' camp, but that's impossible because they stole my uniform and military insignias, I can't even deduce that it would be better if they imprisoned me in an officers' camp, I decided, as there's no way to know what would occur. Then, I saw Lopes enter the room accompanied by the nurse, he teetered, his front was damp with perspiration, his complexion yellow, the nurse seated him, spun around with his enormous elbows and almost knocked over the partition.

As soon as the nurse departed I arose, and, among wrists, ankles, and shoulders, I headed in the direction of the corner where Lopes had been seated, he saw me; he had a fever, which is why they had taken him to the infirmary, he was racked with it and perhaps had a cold, I concluded it was possible for him spread his disease to me, and so I maintained a few steps' distance from my compatriot, I turned my face to the poorly painted wall and, as I stared at the wood slabs that had never been fully painted, he asked me how I felt.

"How do you feel, Captain?"

"Lopes, I already told you, don't call me Captain . . ."

"Yes, my captain, I won't call you Captain again."

"Without the captain part, Lopes!"

"Of course, Captain."

It wasn't worth it, the man was a wreck, and I could see why, despite the distance I'd placed between us, I chose to partially cover my face, he watched me with blood shot eyes, the fever was rotting his brain, he didn't feel well, no one felt well, not even me . . . a miasma was wriggling and coiling around the rooms of the infirmary, it possessed an intense physical presence, anyone who remained there for any significant time was affected.

"Are you also sick, my captain?"

"Certainly, Lopes, certainly!"

"Did you manage to send my letter?" he asked.

"Yes, of course," I responded.

The only possible response; I couldn't tell him the truth given his condition, it was better to lie, it wasn't even a lie, fundamentally, because sooner or later I would end up sending it, all I had to do was find one of the Red Cross sisters, or ask Lang to send it I thought as I fondled the letter in my pocket, without letting myself enter too much in the breathy air, I felt a certain itchiness, a tingling in specific parts of my body, which was, at the same time, difficult to locate, Lopes soon struck up conversation again, spoke of his mother and of food, insisted on the grilled pheasant, for me a nice bowl of bean soup would do, a few crackers, despite having never tried it, he thought of nothing but his grilled pheasant and potatoes, he was similar to my father in that way, anxious to try everything, regardless of the animal, in truth, my father was proud of his desire to have had it all, he'd eat anything that appeared in front of him, he wished, among other things, to eat camel and crocodile, that was my father's personality, willing to travel long distances just to try some meat or fish, on one occasion he traveled to a village tucked deep in the mountains just to eat wild boar, a friend had sent him a telegram saying they'd lassoed a wild boar and my father bolted breathlessly from the house, took three trains and hitched two cart rides, and when he arrived there the meat was already half rotten but he ate it still, just to say he had, given that the meat tasted of urine and rot, he'd told me the meat wasn't good for anything, yet he'd had to try it so he could tell his friends and acquaintances that he had, that's the way my father was. I, for one, was happy to settle for less, and, slowly, I removed myself from Lopes, recoiled a few steps, and scratched myself.

"Where are you going, my captain?"

"I must confirm that my bowl is still beneath my pillow . . . given the sickness in the air . . . But continue on, Lopes, continue on."

I sat myself on the edge of my bed and groped under my rancid pillow, felt the tin bowl, the Frenchman glanced at me for a second or two, the look was brief but I caught it, his greed didn't sneak by me unnoticed, he wanted my bowl . . . and with that leg! . . . for what? He wanted to accumulate, to flaunt his possessions. For naught! Lopes spoke, rambled on about his little lamb, I had already heard it thousands of times, but I didn't interrupt him, it seemed obvious to me that he was delirious and so I lay down full of itchiness and hunger, my companions in captivity.

VII.

I awoke to Lang whispering in my ear and shaking me, I almost fell from the bed, grabbed hold of the headboard, the pillow, the straw mattress, I still had no sheets, Lang was rocking me frantically, his volume rising, he was all but shouting in my ear.

"Dr. Lang, contain yourself, please. Reduce your enthusiasm," I begged, as the entire structure of the bed shook.

I lifted myself and he, satisfied, pushed me through the room, we passed by a sleeping Lopes, and I pointed.

"Does he have a fever, Dr. Lang?"

"A fever? He's burning up, my dear! Absolutely burning up, you see. He's more fever than man now."

We forged ahead and I quickly deduced that the doctor was leading me to his miniscule office, we followed the hallway to its end and came upon the doorway to his workspace, but Lang stopped and, to my surprise, opened a different door to the left, it was the room where we'd left Slingshot, I thought he'd already been buried but I'd been mistaken, the cadaver was still there, with its head pulverized and without any feet!, my situation had changed shape, grown increasingly complicated, the matter at hand was more dangerous than I had surmised . . . An elated Lang entered the room and circled the table multiple times, then lowered himself and produced a box out of which he removed the feet, he wanted to show me a new cutting technique he'd pioneered, a method all his own, revolutionary, clean, the result of which was arteries that appeared as if chopped by the sharpest cleaver on the chopping block, he thought it marvelous, placed the feet on the table next to Slingshot's head—one of the feet, in truth, on top of his head, or what remained of it—opened his arms and launched into a long explanation regarding his methodology, one required a saw with large teeth to cut the bone, and one with short, serrated teeth to excise the veins. He wanted to know what I thought of his new technique, Lang had no regard for my empty stomach, perhaps he didn't remember that I still hadn't eaten, I hadn't stood for *Appel* that morning nor been stationed in front of the cantina with my bowl, but he wanted to know what my opinion was, I didn't have the skills to evaluate his technique, I would've liked very much to have helped, I assured him, however I knew nothing about surgery, Lang wasn't disheartened, he dragged me out of the room, closed the door, kept me close at his side, I did whatever it took not to be in the lead, I didn't like the idea of having him behind me, Lang and his new technique . . . I was in the infirmary, officially registered as ill . . . Schiller had the papers . . . a whack on the head and I'd wake up footless. We entered the office and as soon as we crossed the threshold I glimpsed a somewhat obscured figure in the room, I squinted my eyes, there was no doubt it was a woman.

"I present to you, my wife. Stand up, my dear," Lang said.

It was, indeed, Frau Lang, his infamous wife, she stood up and I saw that she wasn't blonde, she was brunette, and dressed in the attire of the Red Cross, a hoax to enable her to enter the prisoners' camp, an obtuse idea on her husband's part, she stared at me, offered no words, a few moments passed and her husband watched her from the corner of his eye, flared his nostrils, launched in with some shouted German and soon they were locked in battle, the entire office reverberated with the sound, I caught a word here, another there, the doctor had certainly suffered quite a lot of heartbreak because of that woman, it wasn't shocking that he fell quickly to suspicion, mistrust, obsession, all Germans are sexual deviants, even a lowly recruit would give in readily to the most abject perversions, neurasthenia, mental weakness, spiritual relapse, they are a melancholy people, just looking at the German countryside is enough to make one sad, the treetops tremble, the branches strike a stunning contrast against the slate blue sky, the flat land stretches out endlessly and the mountains appear as if plucked from the pages of a fairy tale, quite different from the ravines of my country, hillsides of pebbles and dust with sprouts of stunted collards that hurt to look at, the Germans own entire villas, enormous, impossible, unbelievable properties, centuries earlier some families even staked out entire forests all for themselves, lakes, cows, sheep, horses, ducks, indeed, hectares and hectares of arable land were needed if you wanted to sustain a twenty-five room palace with six ballrooms, a stable, and a spring with cherubs and carp, I had observed them on my travels across Germany, on my way to the privates' camp . . . me, a captain!

Lang seated himself at the table, his wife returned to her chair, they continued arguing, the doctor turned to me, began staring at my feet, I grew scared . . . However, he was once again leaps and bounds ahead of me, because he'd prepared himself to speak exclusively of his wife, was busy remembering his shared past with *Fräulein Altmeier*, that was what he called her, she was no longer Frau Lang to him, certainly not, the two were, at that moment, seated together before me, but in the beginning, when their relationship began in the park by the river, they were no more than friends, Lang's new acquaintance had asked him for help, she was terribly indebted, her father was rich but, due to the shame she had caused them in Hamburg, he wouldn't pay for anything until she arranged a husband, the creditors wouldn't let up, they threw promissory notes in her face, insulted her while at church and whenever she went for a walk, upon entering her house the papers rose all the way to her neck, she had to swim through them to reach the bedroom, it was a constant avalanche, the documents obstructed the door, were strewn across the hallway, tucked snugly between the bedsheets, each drawer contained at minimum ten letters from people she owed money or their legal representatives, requests for large sums, average sums, low sums, she even owed money to the Kaiser himself, Fräulein Altmeier convinced Lang to travel with her, she needed a change of scenery, for which reason they left for Baden-Baden, where they reserved two rooms at the Hotel Simmer. Nothing intimate occurred between them there, a touch of the hand, a grazed dress, Lang had kissed her on the wrist on the riverbank, between bushes and tree branches, but they were nothing more than friends in a public place, anyone could have seen that.

"Nothing more? Just a kiss on the wrist?" my friend in the café asked.

"Yes, yes . . . It happened just as I told you, or close enough. How would I know?"

My friend was curious, myself as well, he wanted to know what time it was, but I didn't ask the waiter, who served us another tea and coffee, I removed a cigarette from my pocket and lit it, the room now smelled of fried food, they dragged chairs and tables around, the plates clinked, it was much noisier than in Baden-Baden, at the Hotel Simmer. The basements at Simmer dated back to the Roman occupation, the Romans were everywhere there was water, the empire was indestructible, it had never ceased to exist, had only changed its name, it had all begun in Babylon . . . In any case, Lang had concocted certain delusions after the riverside wrist kisses, it's not surprising he'd given in, it was his own fault, of course, he'd let himself get carried away, had grown weak, all mere imagination, pure fabrication on his part, Fräulein Altmeier hadn't instigated it, in truth, she'd proven herself entirely placid, a veritable brick wall against his advances, there were no two ways about it, the days passed, and, after some silence, the doctor again approached Fräulein Altmeier, but she didn't even know the man, she hadn't conceded him such intimacies, his imagination had deceived him, what did he want now, what could she do to help him?, nothing, of course, it was pure delusion, there had been no kisses on the wrist, there wasn't even a river, nor a bank, nor trees, nor bushes, nothing at all had occurred, Man is far too prone to fantasy, it's a trick played on us by the soul, imagination is the devil's playground, at times my own dreams seem more real to me than reality, in the mornings

I await the stranger who kissed me, I seek in vain to remember the location I visited one springtime day, I could swear the place belongs to the real world, I live a different kind of life, there's no cure for this ailment, something worth investigating, to discover a medication . . . Lang also dreamed and couldn't even find the river anymore, didn't see it anywhere, Fräulein Altmeier went so far as to agree to accompany him on his quest for the riverbank, a useless expedition as they encountered nothing, absolutely nothing, Fräulein Altmeier continued to have problems, the letters piled up in her house, she had received a telegram from her landlord that she was to be evicted, they'd already called the police, it was impossible to live that way, with the letters cascading down the stairs and onto the floor below, cluttering the building's hallways, plunging them into utter darkness, the floors were completely obscured beneath the papers, a child had even been lost in there, the parents of whom were only able to find it three days later, nearly dead from dehydration with its ears nibbled by rats, enormous rats that had made their nests in the creditors' letters, wallpapered with seizure notices notarized with the imperial seal! And stamps with the emperor's face! And the empress's face! Boats, as well . . . Licked stamps, slimy with slobber. Unbearable, unacceptable . . . To top it all off, the foul smell of carrion, and not just from rats but mid-sized animals, large animals, gigantic animals, massive moles, unnatural aberrations, one had to breathe only through the mouth, avoid using the nose, the stench, the risk of illness, it was enough to infect the whole city, sanitation authorities had inspected the building but hadn't found the source of the pestilence, a neighbor on the third floor had fallen ill, was still bedridden . . . it was too much. Fräulein Altmeier told him this again and then a third time, he already knew all about it, was familiar with the details, he listened to her from near the window of her hotel room, he remained seated in his chair and she on the edge of her bed, they were seated much the same as they were before me now, while I remained standing . . . Lang, however, understood the situation perfectly, it was obvious that the landlord had decided to evict her first and foremost because of the rats, public health concerns, the risk of fire . . . And so he opened his bag and gave her some money. "It's all I have with me," he said.

Fräulein Altmeier stashed the money in her handbag and replied: "Good lord, I'm famished! How about you, Herr Lang?"

He was also hungry, for which reason they headed for Simmer's restaurant and seated themselves at a table; he ordered the soup, Fräulein Altmeier chose the quail with truffle sauce on a bed of asparagus, the hotel served sophisticated cuisine befitting its illustrious guests, Lang had studied in Paris, treated himself only to the best, he ate his soup and waited for his companion to delicately finish her quail, her truffles, and her asparagus, despite the fact that the train he planned to catch departed within the half hour. Afterward, Fräulein Altmeier ordered ice cream with slivered almonds. He wasn't interested in dessert.

"Ah, I've eaten too much," she told him.

She moved her hand to her stomach and made as if to get up, she remained seated, however, and the waiter immediately brought her a tea to aid in digestion, they rose and the waiter extended his hand, Fräulein Altmeier stared at Lang, smiled, he reciprocated the smile and then searched in his pockets, his collar . . . they'd caught him off guard, he'd stored the money in his bag and, following that, had taken the money out of the bag . . . However, he found something in the seat of his pants, a tip, a sorry excuse, quite undignified for a doctor educated in Paris. Afterward, they headed for the hotel gardens, Lang arm in arm with his friend, he seemed apprehensive, he had missed his train and all he could do was catch another one, buy another ticket, damn it all, he had to find a bank, he didn't have a cent on him, and that tip! It seemed to him that the waiter was watching him from the other side of the glazed doors with a mocking grin, he'd become, within the span of a few mere moments, a contemptible customer, had embarrassed himself thoroughly. The future cuckold! If only he had at least been wary . . . Fräulein Altmeier had confided in him certain details about her life, with special attention to her financial dilemmas and her father's ultimatum that he was soon to disown her, but she was preoccupied more than anything with the letters that had accumulated, she would have to find a new place of residence as soon as she returned to the city, a more welcoming home with quieter neighbors, Lang had lost himself in foolish thoughts, here regarding the hotel employee, there regarding the train, I imagined I wouldn't have been able to think easily about anything else given the circumstances. Thankfully, he had already paid for the rooms.

"Listen, my dear Brigitte, wouldn't you be able to lend me a little money for the train?" he asked.

At that moment, they crossed paths with another gentleman, an Austrian who was staying at the Hotel Simmer, Fräulein Altmeier detached herself from Lang and ran to the new arrival, gave him her arm, let out a laugh, and after a few garden ruminations in the footsteps of his friend and the Austrian, Lang barreled forward, ascended the stairs to his room, grabbed his luggage, returned his room key to reception, and headed to the bank where he withdrew the money to buy a new train ticket. He wasn't able to exchange the ticket he'd already bought, not even for a partial refund . . . My friend in the café was horrified, his mouth trembled. Yes, Lang had footed the entire bill . . . The bushes and the trees that he saw from the train struck him

as added costs, they sickened him, all he could do was close his eyes
and await his arrival at his destination, after returning to the city,
Fräulein Altmeier continued to face financial problems, she lacked
the funds to relocate, to buy clothing or food, after all, how could
one work in such conditions? Impossible. Lang helped her gladly,
and she listened to him as they walked in a park far from the banks
of the river, she was terrified of the river, how could he have imagined she could ever have been capable . . . and on the wrist, no less
. . . Yes, he continued seeing Fräulein Altmeier, had created a kind
of routine around it, despite becoming increasingly irritated each
time he saw her, she dragged him to cafes, restaurants, and fabric
warehouses where she would invariably forget her coin purse, her
bag, she was distracted, and would sit and smile as he rummaged
in his pockets, scraped through the dregs . . . I stood there and
absorbed what Lang told me. They were both naturally talkative
individuals, clucking hens! Parrots! I didn't stop listening . . . but
it was, in truth, a miracle that I understood or retained anything
they told me, I hadn't eaten since the day prior, not even a crust, it's
incredible I absorbed the information, I was worn thin for sure, had
lost years off my life, Fräulein Altmeier was a sentimental woman
and saw no issue in harassing him whenever she pleased, Sundays
included! Lang would go to Mass and find her waiting, he'd exit
the station and there she'd be . . . Fräulein Altmeier had moved
to another neighborhood, now lived on a major street close to the
theater, she made use of all the amenities at her disposal there, and
it would be difficult for the road to grow cluttered with letters, however, the doctor couldn't think without her appearing in his path,
always with her complaints, various grievances, one day it was the
boss who tried to seduce her while she was opening a drawer, the
next it was stolen wages.

All the while, Lang was seeking a way to mention the incident in Baden-Baden. He tried to broach the subject with her once more, but quickly stopped himself, how could he be capable of imagining that . . . she would never have spoken to him in a tone that would have permitted him to . . . and on the banks of the river!

He continued to feel perturbed and decided to write to the authorities of Baden-Baden to make an inquiry into the river. He'd sought out maps at the library but found nothing. One morning, the letter he'd been waiting for arrived at the station, the director of the Baden-Baden spa himself assured Lang that there was, indeed, a river in Baden-Baden, it was the river Oos, and that, between the river and the thermal springs, Baden-Baden was made almost entirely of water, at least since the Roman Empire, in truth, Baden-Baden was little more than water, without water Baden-Baden wouldn't even exist, it would be nothing more than a lost harem in the mountains, Baden-Baden is Baden-Baden precisely because of the water, the spa director told him, and the Burgomaster corroborated it in an addendum. Lang was, thus, enlightened regarding the water in Baden-Baden. On top of the addendum from the Burgomaster, the spa director had also extended Lang the kindness of attaching a clipping to the letter from the local paper, the *Baden Zeitung*, containing an article on the enormous trout fished in the river Oos, the title of which was "Munich Visitor Catches Meter-Long Trout," or something to that effect.

A shock. Lang was floored, began to think frequently of his own death, would gaze at the train tracks and then at his feet, but in the end made no decision, time passed and he didn't throw himself over, himself or Fräulein Altmeier, it was incredible how he would have been entirely capable of kissing her on the wrist once again and, simultaneously, of seeing her savaged by a locomotive . . . Oh, how marvelous a Fräulein Altmeier squashed by a train would be, her head to one side, her body to the other, such earthly delights. Despite her difficulties and the sadness she endured, she had life in a death grip. Her problems pursued her, the letters began to accumulate in her new home and a cat had already disappeared among the service obligations and credit notes, the owner had searched for it in vain, even going so far as to request the aid of a retired military man who lived down the road, who released his pinscher in Fräulein Altmeier's small apartment, but it too disappeared. Following that, they tried to find the cat and the pinscher using the resources of the police commissioner's mastiff, the mastiff smelled the papers, barked, launched itself into the documents, another bark was heard, two barks, a yowl, and then it was gone. The house quickly became uninhabitable. Lang visited Fräulein Altmeier and noted that the situation was indeed grave, he found himself imagining her lost among all those envelopes, but even so, would have been capable of kissing her right there, on top of all those papers . . . They sat, each in their own chair, at times glancing at the mountain of letters that threatened to swallow them at any moment.

"Fräulein Altmeier, you won't believe the contents of a letter I received recently," Lang said.

"Ah, Herr Lang, a letter," Fräulein Altmeier responded.

"Yes, yes, a letter," he affirmed.

"I haven't read a letter in months. I've given up on it!" she told him.

"Of course, not surprising . . . But imagine this, I received a letter from the spa director at Baden-Baden. And with an addendum from the Burgomaster."

"The Burgomaster!"

"Yes, yes, of Baden-Baden, my dear Fräulein."

"Oh! Incredible."

"But listen here, please. Do you know what the spa director wrote to me? That there is a river in Baden-Baden called the Oos. Indeed, Baden-Baden wouldn't exist without the river Oos, were it not for that river, Fräulein Altmeier, Baden-Baden would be a miserable hamlet. A half dozen cows and a few goats, do you see? And the wind whipping through the hills. All confirmed by the Burgomaster."

"How fantastic!"

"Now, the most fantastic is that the Oos, same as any river, has two banks, do you understand? A river must necessarily have two banks, because if it didn't, it wouldn't be a river, it could be a lake or a quagmire, but never a river, no. But in Baden-Baden there is a river, Fräulein Altmeier, are you following me? Perhaps there is also a quagmire, I don't know. However, it is certain that there exists a river and that it has two banks."

"Herr Lang, you are so learned; you even correspond with spa directors."

"The Burgomaster also replied to me."

"Of course. You're so learned . . . Have you already seen this promissory note I have here, Herr Lang?"

The doctor read a few of the creditors' notes strewn about the living room and before he knew it, he was back out on the street, and damn it all, he had lent her more money; he didn't even know how it happened . . . in the middle of all those papers, his wallet had been emptied . . . and he'd taken with him a few creditors' notes whose due dates were approaching . . . had he signed some document? There was nothing to do, he could only continue onward to the hospital. Once there, he threw the creditors' notes in the air, put on then stripped off his frock, and punched the wall . . . Some of the patients waiting to be seen were startled by the sound and soon the department head was knocking on Lang's office door . . . He entered and got straight to the point: Lang had to compose himself, this was not behavior becoming of a doctor, and one who had studied with Dr. Leclerc-Armand, no less, the rumors regarding Lang's romantic life were numerous, the department head seated himself in the master's chair and counseled Lang that he should be careful with the young woman, he felt a certain empathy for Lang, considered him a good doctor, a resourceful individual, and responsible, his only inability seemed to be in handling women, and he had resolved, therefore, to explain to Lang what to do.

"The first step is to eliminate all contact with this woman."

"Yes, yes!" Lang chirped.

At that instant, he showed the department head the creditors' notes and, following that, the letter he had received from Baden-Baden.

"Look, sir, the river Oos crosses through Baden-Baden, which wouldn't exist without it . . . and it has two banks. Do you see?"

"Yes, naturally!"

The doctor was overly excited, and the department head tried to calm him so that he might continue with his recommendations, Lang, however, wouldn't be mollified and began to take apart one of the many gadgets he had stored with such care around his office, metal pieces, rivets, screws, glass boxes flew across the room . . . For a long time prior he'd felt he was losing control. In the end, the department head gave him a smack and forced him to sit in his chair. He also ordered Lang to take up a pencil and some paper, as he would explain to him thereafter exactly how to solve his problem.

He sent a letter, and on the following day he was visited by Fräulein Altmeier, who was in the middle of some crisis, the police commissioner's mastiff had reappeared, horribly skinny and barely able to stand, it had emerged from the papers and leaned against the wall, then laid down and sighed, it was entirely depleted, the commissioner was moved almost to tears when he saw it, Lang removed his remaining pile of cash from a drawer and gave it to Fräulein Altmeier, who then stored the money in her handbag, it was a very practical handbag, spacious yet small, much like wartime pockets, they possessed an extraordinary sense of spaciousness and tidiness, this is how you build a country, an empire, really, and they sealed the deal. Afterward, they married, thus fulfilling the department head's suggestions, a madman, he'd disgraced himself on that man's accord! Because of his advice . . . Lang sighed and stared at the floor.

Soon the woman addressed me:

"*Sprechen Sie Deutsch?*"

She didn't speak French.

"*Nur ein bisschen . . .*" I responded.

It was all she needed to begin her screed; much like her husband, she had a disruptive effect on the calm in the room, obliterated any silence . . . That war was a steady stream of attacks against silence, weapons, explosives, shouts, and words that wounded, I didn't understand half of what she said, something about a garden, a house . . . She spoke much too fast for my grasp of the language, and also much too loud, I had never heard a German speak at such volume, her voice reverberated off the tent walls, it was very disgraceful . . . Lang hung his head, didn't look up from the ground, the man was beset, he had endured her for years, had spent a lifetime listening to her shout in cafes, in restaurants, at the hospital, he was used to it, had acquired a special taste for it, they shared an intimate relationship . . . She talked without stopping and I nodded, moved my head up and down, I didn't understand half of what she told me, however, I had to continue the spectacle, to withstand the sonic onslaught . . . Then, while his wife was still speaking, Lang shoved his hand into his inside coat pocket and removed some papers.

"Now look here, my friend," he said to me in French, and turning to his wife: "*Sehen Sie!*"

She leered at the papers, didn't even move her neck, nor did she respond to him, but instead continued conversing with me, something about a chair, I believe . . .

"*Herre Gott!*" shouted Lang, who was all stopped up and ready to explode, he shook the papers, it was the letter from the Baden-Baden spa director and the addendum from the Burgomaster, he demonstrated them to me, they proved the existence of the river Oos and its banks . . . according to him . . . "*Hier Sehen Sie, mein Herr . . .*"

He wanted me to analyze them in detail, I spoke little German and read even less, however, I said nothing. A closed mouth! Without compromising myself. Fräulein Altmeier was discussing a Christmas nativity play, I'd venture, the Kaiser . . . He held the papers in front of her face, and yet she saw nothing, she was deep in her own conversation, I had lost the thread after the Kaiser, and Lang, red-faced and puffy, wouldn't cease showcasing his papers, he entreated me, the office filled with French and German words to such an extent that maybe it wouldn't withstand the confrontation, maybe it was about to collapse . . . It was a ferocious feud. The doctor had put himself through a lot on account of that woman, had even showed up to work with a black eye after taking a beating from a gentleman in defense of her honor, she never made good choices, always involved herself with perverse individuals, deviants of the worst variety, the Dutchman being a prime example, she'd taken off with one of them to Bukovina. To Bukovina! I almost asked him if he thought of emigrating to Papua New Guinea, however, I held back, it was best to remain quiet and watch the spectacle unfold.

At that point in his retelling, Lang was frothing at the mouth, it had happened years prior, yet it continued to excite him, because she swore she had no knowledge of anything, that in all reality Lang had hallucinated everything, he was prone to fantasy . . .

"All for a woman who is incapable of saying she's sorry, Monsieur! She can't do it, I tell you. And for what, really? There's always some reason."

Fräulein Altmeier continued her monologue, and Lang, by the looks of it, was unsatisfied, he tossed the yellowed letters from Baden-Baden on the table and rose from his chair.

"Look, this hag could talk for a week straight without stopping and without listening to a word from anyone else. She's a lout. And refuses to pay attention to me, even if I toss myself to the ground at her feet!"

Then, Lang threw himself to the ground, and with unexpected aplomb for a man of his age, he fell flat on his back yet he didn't cry out, and soon set himself to rolling around in the dirt contorting himself for his wife, who, nevertheless, continued speaking, something about a horse, he was splayed out, yes, and neighed, hee-haw, hee-haw, hee-haw, later he yelped and yowled. Aaaoooooooh. At long last, Fräulein Altmeier (or Frau Lang!), in her little Red Cross dress, went quiet and stared.

"*Schwein!*" she shouted.

Following that, Lang brayed loud and clear, and the office shuddered, I remained quiet, he certainly was a pig, they all were, I had nothing to do with any this, it was none of my business . . . The woman picked up her lecture where she'd left off, this time with a word or two in French thrown in, she wanted me to understand, desperate to assuage any remaining doubts. She was orating regarding an old fiancé, it seemed. Lang had sought her out, pursued her, and she was engaged, *mit einem anderen Mann*, he was a pervert, yes ma'am, the lot of them, a band of perverts . . .

He stood up, again with aplomb, he must have already been used to making similar scenes, the spectacle didn't end, it was impossible to stop . . . Without losing myself deep in thought, the love they shared was evident. Lang was a hysteric neurotic, and his wife a possible narcissist . . . she was most certainly a narcissist, she prattled on, alleged that, aside from being a pig, he was also a coward, hadn't ever gotten ahead in life because of *peur du succès*, she said it like that, in French. He sat beside her, breathless. After a moment of silence, a renewed altercation arose between them, they hurled accusations at one another in German and I hardly understood anything, besides, I was starving and lost focus, it was too intimate, I limited myself to observing them, I was tired, exhausted, sapped, I stared at the door, it was so near, I slinked forward, one foot and then the other, they didn't even notice my absence, I reached the door and continued down the hallway, I didn't cross paths with any nurses or guards, and I exited.

I breathed the fresh, hot air, it smelled sweet, I stopped by a bush that hedged the infirmary building and spotted a robin, which drew near. Explosions erupted in the distance, I followed the robin easily, that area of Germany was very walkable, the land was entirely flat, one has to admit that here, in my country, you go up and down, one slope, two slopes, a hill, some stairs, endless steps that at once grow larger only to straighten out again, walking downhill is tiresome!, it's ridiculous, I'm a jester, a buffoon, it seems I do nothing but descend and ascend for the entertainment of others. Out there, I followed the robin over the flat yard's battered earth. The bird chirruped.

VIII.

My friend in the café was ready for lunch, it was that hour and he was feeling peckish, the plates and serving trays filled the room with vaporous smells, the waiter approached us once again to inform us of the daily specials, and of the flower seller's ultimate departure, or, at least, that was his belief, he had yet to see her again, she'd disappeared, nothing more than a few petals and leaves scattered across the walkway in front of the café's large display window, which opened out onto the street, any passerby could see us seated there, beset by the teapots and teacups that the waiter now deposited onto his tray, the smell of fried foods at first caused me agony, but soon piqued my appetite, I, too, announced my desire for lunch, the waiter fumbled with the tableware, the dining room was full, his colleague was attending other customers, all of whom were in a hurry, the teapot almost teetered off and crashed to the ground, he insisted on the dining room in back, it was much more discrete, an exclusive dining area for select clientele, he would serve us lunch there if we so desired, but only and exclusively if that was our wish, he beseeched us to put it to him plainly if we intended to be served in the room in back, my friend was hungry, I was as well, I had lost my patience with the waiter, if I'm being quite honest I don't feel that I lost my patience because I was hungry, I believe it was because I had grown impatient, yes, because of the teapot that had almost fallen, perhaps it wouldn't have irritated me to see it shattered to pieces on the ground, or placed firmly on the tray, but the oscillating motion had made me hotheaded, at the time I wasn't aware what had caused my irritation, in part because I was distracted, I was recalling the prisoners' camp in Germany and the hunger I'd felt on my first day in the infirmary, however I quickly became aware that it was the teapot that had irritated me, I think, and I thus acquiesced to the waiter's suggestion, and my friend agreed, we would dine in the back room, an area the likes of which had never before been seen in the world of fine dining, assuming lunch wouldn't take too long . . . We followed him down a dark hallway and entered a room whose windows looked over a small garden patio of dry, wilted flowers, in peak growing season no less, how shameful . . . The waiter asked us immediately to choose a table, the room was empty, we observed the tables and chairs and I saw, in that instant, an aquarium, to which I drew near; my friend accompanied me.

"Here is the novelty, gentlemen! There are people who visit us just to see this fabulous aquarium, it is an incredible invention, we have saltwater fish, my good sirs, saltwater fish, they're not from the river, no, they come straight from our beaches," said the waiter, who then departed.

Swimming in the aquarium's muddy, dark-green water were four or five fish, one of them had suctioned its mouth to the glass and seemed to be staring, another swam sideways, as if half of its body had just died, a victim, no doubt, of apoplexy, I did a half turn to summon the waiter and point out the fish to him, but we were already alone in the dining area for select clientele, the waiter had left, my friend said nothing, he continued to stare at the aquarium, I also observed it now with redoubled attention and spotted another creature, a lobster lurking in the shadow of the algae that grew on the glass, an aquatic jungle of mosses and verdigris, sludge and stagnant, infected water, probably a mixture of tap water and saltwater they had brought from the ocean in buckets, yes, there were indeed buckets in the little garden, and it seemed to me they were lined with saltpeter, disgusting, not to mention that the lobster was missing one of its claws . . . I circled the aquarium, stared at the lobster from every angle, it continued lacking a claw, didn't have the left one, and the waiter had disappeared. One day we will pay for what we do to animals, I said to my friend, the day will come when we are confronted by our relationship to nature, I assured him, in the future, I said, we will be forced to live with the actions we take against animals and the environment. People disregard their responsibilities and a time will come when they'll no longer be able to, I guaranteed him, these days, there are people who don't accept their responsibility for living things, however, one day they will be forced to confront it; in my mind, a person with an elevated sense of art isn't worth anything if they have no respect for nature, a person who disrespects nature will never be deserving of my sympathy, I commented, even if they have a great understanding of art and culture, which are held by many as Man's greatest feats, as much as someone might show me paintings, books, or sculptures—which are considered the greatest of Human achievement—I will never feel for them even the slightest esteem if they don't respect nature and accept their responsibility for it, I promised him. Afterward, the waiter appeared, and I asked him if, instead of bringing us the daily special, he might serve us the lobster and at a discount, as it was missing a claw.

We sat, my friend insisted on hearing the story of how my voice was recorded, reaffirmed his great interest in the recording as he shoved his hand in his pocket and confirmed he was still in possession of the two train tickets, it was difficult to garner his interest in other stories, because the one about my voice captivated him above all else, I'm sure he wanted to brag that he knew the first man from Portugal to ever have his voice recorded, at least the first man from Portugal who wasn't a singer, that's why he dwelled on the story so often. I tried to remember the day of the recording in all its detail, the hunger pinched my stomach, although not so much as on that day, the one after I was admitted to the infirmary. I had been interned there the day prior, I told him, the scientists arrived at the end of the day on which I was admitted to the hospital, I said, and as such the recordings only began on the following day, had the phonologists arrived earlier perhaps the recordings would have begun precisely on the day Lang installed me in a bed in the infirmary, but the truth is that they arrived only at the end of the day and dined with Schiller, and given that they didn't record my voice on the first day of my internment, I told him, I went hungry for many hours. I wandered between the infirmary and the bushes on the other side of the fence under the cover of the conjugal discussion occurring in Lang's office, the robin took flight, the building elongated, the wooden boards inflated with air then quickly returned to their previous size, this repeated time and again before my eyes, I doubted what I was seeing as I felt ready to collapse and propped myself up against the wall, but it was true, the planks were growing larger and longer without stopping beneath the Lang couple's forceful shouts . . . They ate three meals a day, four maybe, they had grown strong on military rations and had no lack of air . . . I stuck my fingers directly between the planks that grew and shrank and I felt nothing, incredible!, the boards squeezed my fingers and I didn't even wail, the situation didn't bode well, it would be difficult for me to speak to the Germans' gadgets and knickknacks if I proved myself incapable of wailing when my fingers were squeezed between the boards of Lang's office, I would be expelled from the infirmary, the shouting increased in volume and, simultaneously, seemed to move farther away . . . I sharpened my ears and looked around.

"Hey!" shouted a guard.

He wanted to know what I was doing over there, if I would be so kind, as well as what was going on . . . I wasn't in front of Lang's office at all, but at a wall where I had inserted my hand, I also had a cigarette between my middle and pointer finger, I was startled, dropped the cigarette, it fell on the opposite side of the fence, I squatted down and reached out, tried to bring it back through the fence but couldn't do it, the German screamed, he was furious at seeing me there, feared I'd wither away, evaporate into the air above the camp, I didn't give up, I took a branch and tried to pull the cigarette toward me, the guard drew nearer, spat, was at that point unintelligible, a few meters away Timóteo and Costa were preening each other like monkeys among a group of prisoners, seated in the sun like that they really did look like primates, they established social relations just like the monkeys my father had once taken me to see at a park along the river, who had roared above the sounds of the lion, their cries echoing throughout the city, we are simians, oh yes, and the guard salivated, frothed at the corners of his mouth, threatened me with the tip of his bayonet, he feared I would escape through the fence, my fingers really were high-tailing it out of there, freedom plunged into me through my nailbeds, he raised his rifle, ready to jab it into my chest, I recoiled my arm and used it to shield my face, but then I heard someone speaking muddled German, it was Le Bidon, he had run to my aid from the circle of primates with a cigarette in one hand, he offered it immediately to the Kraut, all but placed it in the corner of the man's sopping mouth, they became fast friends, the guard departed, Le Bidon was still panting from his run, he was exhausted, had proved himself a true friend, and then crouched down. He lowered himself to my level, what with the vertigo and my head spinning, drew close and, in a whisper, asked if I had delivered the package to Lang, if the package was safe in the infirmary, he couldn't ask him personally, didn't want to attract attention, wouldn't dream of entering the sick house, he was preoccupied with the little paper-wrapped object, perhaps there were two, or maybe even three paper-wrapped objects, I hadn't opened it, it was still stored in my boot, I had hidden it in my left boot where there was no lack of storage, both of my feet would have fit easily in there, the prison diet wasn't entirely devoid of advantages, however I told him that yes, I had delivered it to Lang, as soon as I'd seen him I'd delivered it, do you really think I wouldn't have given it to him the moment we met?, I asked Le Bidon, despite having the package hidden in my boot. Then, there was a roar, and the sky ripped open.

"*Die Franzosen!*" someone cried.

Le Bidon went pale . . . It was planes, two Frenchmen in pursuit of a German. The Kraut seemed to fall apart in midair, he was trapped among the wires, we heard bullets striking the roof of the Kommandantur.

"One of them's gonna crash, gonna crash," shouted another prisoner in English. Le Bidon grew even more terrified and shook.

There was an intense whirring, a boom, some dust exited from the buildings . . . A few minutes later I couldn't even hear my thoughts, nor could I see farther than the wooden boards and bricks on the ground, some whole bricks and others that had been reduced to red dust were scattered about with a few men mixed in, the rumbling of the crumbling walls completely muffled the bruumm of the French planes and an enormous dust cloud billowed out before me, I was forced to close my eyes and when I reopened them the field was silent except for a few coughs, a groan or two, there were boards everywhere, the plane's wing was burning on top of one half of the infirmary, debris . . . Le Bidon appeared in front of me covered in dust, he was red from head to toe, he shook himself and the dust scattered, he tried to speak, his throat was dry, he coughed.

"And the package . . ." he said.

The package indeed!

"D'you have any food? I'd eat anything," I said.

I hadn't eaten all day . . . He, however, said nothing, coughed again, I turned my back to him and headed for the infirmary, I was barely able to stand, I took a few steps and noticed the sorry state the building had been reduced to, half of it had been toppled while the other half appeared to have emerged unscathed, the Lang couple was standing at the door, the doctor wiped off the documents sent by the Burgomaster from Baden-Baden, Frau Lang seemed to me somewhat frozen in her Red Cross attire, I thought of mentioning my lack of provisions to Lang, or asking if he was well. In the end, I said something else.

"Have you seen Lopes?"

"How could I have seen him? Just you tell me that!" he retorted, advancing over the bricks and debris, and drawing nearer.

Then, Commander Schiller emerged from who knows where, accompanied by two soldiers and wearing an impeccable suit, he began to speak and, from what I understood, was complaining of a certain burning smell hanging in the air, the doctor cleaned the red dust from his face just as Schiller kicked some bricks, bits of zinc, and metallic fragments, Lang responded *Ja, Herr Direktor*, Schiller didn't remain there, he was possessed, was squawking under the pressure of the camp visitors' imminent arrival, thankfully the Kommandantur had only had its roof damaged, a few shingles punctured and nothing more . . . But there were wounded! Afterward, he grew quiet and seemed ready to depart with his escort, however he stopped, did a half turn and faced me, I was still covered in red dust, I hadn't even tried to clean my face, I sneezed, coughed, he grumbled something or other and then he left.

"What did he say?" I asked Lang.

"I don't know!" he said.

He didn't know. Following that, we rejoined the men writhing in the debris. It did, indeed, smell of burning. While we searched for Lopes among the rubble, Lang spoke of the recording that would begin that afternoon or on the following day, it was to be a revolutionary investigation, one that would alter the course of human history, end war, each man would be able to understand the other, his wife walked around us, that one nobody could shut up, Lang quickly grew irritated, interrupted her by wielding a rock . . . In the end, Lopes emerged from the rubble and didn't appear to be wounded, just somewhat confused.

"My captain!"

Lopes looked up as Lang braved an avalanche of words, there was an intense whirring, and from the walls some more dust emerged . . .

"Lopes, I already asked you not to call me captain, you are well aware I don't have the necessary documentation to prove my rank . . ."

"What did you say, my captain?"

"I told you not to call me captain!"

"What?" he asked over the din.

In order to verify that he had indeed emerged unharmed, I asked him to tell me what day it was.

"But do you want to know the day of the week or the day of the month, my captain?"

In truth, I was indifferent. Week or month, he didn't know either, and dates, whichever you prefer, are an abstraction . . . I asked him his name, what his age was, where he came from. I have to admit he knew how to speak on all those subjects, albeit slowly and with numerous halting pauses. Lang proposed observing his tongue, seeing if he could roll it up in his mouth, if it appeared normal in all its aspects. Lopes leaned on me and we both beat the dust off him with our palms . . . I smacked wrists and ankles, he complained of aches and pains, cried out with each whack, however, we continued and a red cloud soon formed that obscured Lang completely. Afterward, the German coughed for a long while, I began to worry he would never stop, then he emerged from the cloud and also set about patting the dust off his own clothes. Lopes continued to complain. With the dust finally cleared I was able to inspect him fully, and what I saw wasn't pretty, a gash in his head revealed his brain, I saw it pulsate, a gray-pink mass palpitating in Lopes' head . . . I motioned to Lang, who placed himself at my side and also saw the mass shudder, even Frau Lang saw it, she brought a handkerchief to her mouth, the hankie bearing the Red Cross insignia, it was much too horrific a spectacle for a woman, Lopes complained and began removing his coat, which came apart in tatters, soon all that remained were the sleeves, the Portuguese uniform, disposable and hygienic, Frau Lang tried to cover him with her handkerchief, the doctor's wife was a humanist, after all, but it didn't cover much more than a few bones, Lopes had been forgetting to eat lately, not surprising given the gray-pink mass beating in his cranium, his ideas floated off into the air and Lang sighed, grabbed the handkerchief, and covered the massive gash on his head, then ordered him to lie down on what remained of a bed. I translated what the German required, and Lopes lay down immediately on his right side, and bleated.

"Did you send the letters, my captain?" he stammered, the handkerchief pulsating.

"Yes, of course, Lopes, don't worry," I told him as I touched the pocket where I had stored the letters, Lopes's and Almeida's, I assured him that I'd sent the letter with the volunteers who brought crackers, while in truth, the letter was in my pocket along with Almeida's, but I guaranteed him that yes, I had sent it. He grew calmer.

"My sheep, Captain."

"Yes, Lopes, your little lamb! It is well!"

"My head hurts, Captain . . ."

"Not for long, the doctor will take care of you."

"Thank you, Captain, thank you, white roses are the most beautiful . . ." He was hallucinating.

"Yes, Lopes, of course they are, but don't overextend yourself, you must still visit Papua New Guinea, there are no lack of flowers there."

"Do you think so, Captain? You think I'll make it out of here?"

"Of course."

He was hallucinating! He spoke of roses with that mass inflating and deflating in his head . . . I patted him on the shoulder, gave him some encouragement, the dust rose, half the room was still standing, I backed up a little, stepped on something, it was the Frenchman, my bed neighbor, he was curled up and trembling on the floor, it was a hot day and yet he shivered, the Langs picked up their conversation where they'd left it, I removed the doctor, we stepped over the remains of a toppled wall, Lang was indignant about the aerial combat, it was becoming increasingly frequent, he spoke of armistice, but given the ammunitions, the end of the war seemed incalculable . . . his wife shouted, he grabbed a board and threw it at her, she ran, and we were left in peace.

"What do you require, *mein Herr*?" he asked.

I pointed to Lopes, Lang twisted his mouth, a look of repugnance,

I lowered myself and removed the package Le Bidon had given me, the doctor smiled.

"*Ja, ja.*"

He was satisfied, he stored the package in his frock and dragged me outside the infirmary, smiled, clicking his tongue with a dry sound, I found it strange that we were leaving the infirmary given the large number of complaints occurring around us and I inquired about Lopes, it surprised me that we were leaving him there stretched out among the wounded, dust, and debris, if it hadn't all struck me as odd, I would never have asked him; however, I did find it strange and so I asked, and he told me there was nothing we could do, he lacked the supplies as well the time, and in any case, it was pointless, Lopes was *kaputt*, irreversibly lost. I followed him. Frau Lang wasted no time in rejoining, she had been waiting at the door, the nurses and a few guards carried the wounded outside with the aid of some prisoners, the infirmary had sustained more damage than any other building, the plane's wing had sliced the yard down its middle, ripped a gash in the earth, the fuselage sizzled near the fence, I glimpsed my compatriots, Le Bidon was rifling through the unconscious wounded's clothing, Müller as well, the smell of burning spread out across the entire camp, some pieces smoldered in front of the Kommandantur, Schiller eyed us from the window, the Langs picked up the pace, he shouted at her, she stopped, I did too, I turned to the east, my shadow extended to the fence, the shouting grew louder, the birds sang, I didn't hear them, only the cries and moans of the metal contorting over the fire, Frau Lang departed, her back turned to us, Lang came to me and asked what I would do; Schiller appeared, he was angry, I shouldn't be walking around there if I was sick, I had to take care of my throat, he shouted, furious, and Lang pulled me by the arm, I didn't move. I leered at him, and then accompanied him to the infirmary.

My friend wanted to know what happened next, what I sang and spoke for the German recording device the following day; he insisted on that story even though I was honing my silence, it was the only one that truly interested him, he wanted to know what I'd done, what Lang and Schiller had said to me, and, later, the phonologists. I thought of telling him everything right that instant, but I stopped myself, brusquely halted the conversation, my friend wanted a faithful story without any gaps, a concise narration of how the recording had occurred, I had disappointed him and thought, for a few moments, of doing as he wished, but I didn't, I remained hesitant, waited, silent, because, in that instant, the flower seller emerged from the garden behind the restaurant, she appeared in the garden without my knowing how she had entered, had she scaled the wall or did she have a gate key?, perhaps the gate had been left open, but she emerged in front of the window, carrying with her a bouquet of white roses.

JOÃO REIS (1985) is a Portuguese writer and a literary translator of Scandinavian languages. He studied philosophy and has lived in Portugal, Norway, Sweden, and the UK. Reis's work has been compared to that of Hamsun and Kafka, and represents a literary style unseen in contemporary Portuguese writing. His novel *Bedraggling Grandma with Russian Snow* (Corona/Samizdat, Slovenia, 2021) was shortlisted for the Fernando Namora Award and longlisted for the 2022 Dublin Literary Award. *The Devastation of Silence*, his third novel, was longlisted for Prémio Oceanos 2019.

ADRIAN MINCKLEY has a BA in Social Theory from the Evergreen State College, and an MA in Literary Translation Studies from the University of Rochester. Her translations have appeared in *Firmament*, *Two Lines Journal*, Words Without Borders, and *Your Impossible Voice*. She received a 2021 PEN/Heim Translation Grant for her work on Márcia Barbieri's *The Whore* (forthcoming from Sublunary Editions, 2023.)

CPSIA information can be obtained
at www.ICGtesting.com
Printed in the USA
BVHW051532211022
649935BV00004B/18